HERE COMES THE HOMICIDE

HERE COMES THE HOMICIDE

ERIN SCOGGINS

HELIUM PRESS

For my parents,
with all my love and appreciation.

1

In the South, we use our manners for good instead of evil.

Most of the time.

If a hurricane's coming, we pull in the lawn furniture before it torpedoes through our neighbor's leaded glass parlor window. If someone dies, we bake their family a casserole loaded with cream-of-something soup and an entire bag of shredded cheddar. And if we pass a broken-down car on the side of a Flat Falls road, we stop and help. No questions asked.

Unless the stranded motorist is from Big River. Then we drive by and toss them a merry wave as we blow past them on the highway.

It's an unspoken rule around these parts. Manners be darned—if you're from Big River, you're the enemy. Which is unfortunate, because I came from Big River. Or rather, my father did.

I had just spent the last hour cruising down every street and circling every parking lot in Flat Falls, searching for my latest bride, who was last seen racing through the town square in her wedding dress. And since I was unable to locate her in town, that meant I was about to cross over into uncharted territory.

Big River.

"She should be easy to spot, Glory," my aunt Beverlee said, her honeyed drawl echoing through my phone's speaker. "She looks like a sparkly marshmallow in that gown."

"Ten bucks says she made a run for it," I replied.

It was tacky for the wedding planner to bet against the marriage before the union even began, but I couldn't help myself. When the bride bolted from her final dress fitting and refused to answer her phone, my visions of a fairy tale ending took a high-speed nosedive into the nearest Carolina swamp. Some brides were tougher than others, and Ruby Fowler, daughter of the Flat Falls mayor and beloved home-town girl, was one of the toughest.

As I approached the bridge between Flat Falls and Big River, I squinted at the rusted red pickup truck with smoke billowing from beneath its hood. I slowed my beat-up Honda to a respectable twenty miles an hour as I cruised past, giving the vehicle a once-over to decide if it was some-body from Flat Falls or if I was going to toot my horn and drive on by.

I recognized the bumper sticker first. It featured a line drawing of the mayor's round face and his latest campaign slogan that read, "*Life is short. Don't die until you vote for Moe.*"

"I found her," I told Beverlee. "She's driving Moe's truck."

"Rookie mistake. Next time, she needs to choose a reli-able escape vehicle. Her father's truck is just as likely to explode as it is to get her out of town."

I pulled to the side of the road and disconnected the

phone. But when I got out of my car and approached the truck, the cab was empty.

Out of the corner of my eye, I saw a flash of white, and I whipped my head around to investigate.

Standing there in her underwear, heaving what appeared to be a pillowy mass of wedding gown into the swirling water below, was Ruby Fowler.

But it wasn't her tangled light brown hair or the dark streaks of mascara smudging her cheeks that had me in a panic. It was the mud puddle soaking into the fabric of her train as she dragged it down the bridge to find a better launching spot.

"Ruby," I said, grabbing the dress before it snagged on one of the seagull stakes jutting up from the railing. I shoved a layer of lace out of the way and looked at my watch. "It's nine in the morning, and your wedding is in a week. Why are you standing on the bridge in your bra instead of sipping mimosas at the bridal salon?"

She gave a defiant sniffle and snaked her fingers around the hem of the dress, only dropping it to pop up a middle finger at a passing motorist who blasted his horn and shouted catcalls out his open window.

I shrugged out of my cardigan and wrapped it around her shoulders, struggling to tuck the dress under one arm while guiding her across the street toward my waiting car.

"Leave it," she insisted, bobbing her chin toward the dress. "String it from the top of the tallest ship you can find. I want it to be a warning."

"A warning?" Barely disguised impatience made my left eye twitch. "About what?"

Ruby and I went through school together, but she left town not long after graduation for a fashion design stint in New York City. While I was busy marrying a loser, she was attending fancy parties and rubbing elbows with celebrities.

She returned to Flat Falls a few years back, opening a clothing boutique, and everybody celebrated her homecoming like she had discovered a cure for the common cold or a vending machine that spit out free hundred-dollar bills. Since then, she had been featured on the cover of *Beach Weekly* half a dozen times and was the recipient of the Miss Flat Falls sash twice.

On top of that, she was marrying an up-and-coming restauranteur who looked like he was straight out of an ad for high-dollar whiskey.

I couldn't see what she had to complain about.

"A warning about men," she said through clenched teeth as she clamped her fingers around the gown. "They ruin everything."

She wasn't the first bride who had complained that having a groom made her wedding more complicated, and I doubted she'd be the last. But I was contract-bound to get her to the altar, so I gave her a gentle smile. "Surely it's not that bad."

Ruby yanked at the dress, and I squeezed my arm in toward my side to keep her from getting it. She might be mad, but this dress was custom sewn by one of the hottest designers in the world, and I wasn't about to let her ruin a piece of imported raw silk that cost more than my car. And hers.

I nodded toward the smoking pickup truck in a last-ditch effort to divert her attention away from the dress she was bent on destroying. "Did you overheat?"

She shrugged, finally releasing her grip on the fabric. "I was in a hurry. Daddy's old truck doesn't respond well when you rush."

That figured. As mayor, Moe Fowler ran everything in Flat Falls like a slow bucket of blueberry syrup. The last time I went into his office for an event permit, I spent the better part of the afternoon pretending to admire Ruby's baby pictures over a glass of hand-pressed lemonade.

Which, come to think of it, was how I ended up as her wedding planner. Moe thought that because I had known Ruby since our mothers shopped for matching white wicker nursery furniture together, I'd be the perfect choice to plan his baby girl's big day.

Well, that, and the fact that the only other wedding planner in the area had bullied Ruby throughout high school, and the mayor held her personally responsible for a large percentage of his daughter's therapy bills.

We made it to my car, and I slipped the dress into the trunk before ushering a sniffling Ruby to the passenger seat. "What could be so awful that it would make you destroy a couture gown?"

She sheepishly glanced back toward the trunk. Even a freaked-out bride knew the value of a beautiful dress. "Is it all right?"

"It's nothing a bleach pen and a steamer can't handle."

It was a lie, of course. Ruby's gown was topped with an intricate tangle of beading and feathers, and it would take more than a washing machine to fix it.

But I didn't tell her that. Instead, I spoke in hushed tones on the drive back and took corners with extra care to keep her from diving back into the tizzy that had led her to the bridge in the first place.

When I parked in front of the Flat Falls municipal building where her father worked, she dropped her head into her hands. "I can't go in there right now."

I pasted on a smile and pointed down the street toward Carolina Weddings' hot pink awning, which jutted out at an awkward angle and had been dangling over the entrance of the pawnshop next door since a tropical storm blew it askew a few weeks earlier. "You're welcome to come hang out with me until you get your bearings."

I motioned down her exposed legs. "And I'm sure we can find something for you to wear. Or I could swing back over to the bridal shop and pick up anything you left behind during your fitting. Like your clothes."

Ruby winced. "That's going to be embarrassing, especially with all those people milling about for the festival."

Ruby's wedding was perfectly scheduled to coincide with the Flat Falls Founder's Day Festival, which long-time residents not-so-secretly referred to as the Roadkill Jubilee, a two-week extravaganza that celebrated the bumpy start of our little town.

The festival had been going on for as long as I could remember. When I was a child, tables of homemade baked goods lined the streets and kids paraded on their bikes. But convinced the town needed to get hipper this year, the mayor had invited food trucks from as far away as Raleigh to join the fun, and more than a dozen of them lined up along the waterfront.

I gestured toward the larger-than-life bronze pig statue in front of the building. Earl presided over the downtown area like a giant, his porcine belly wider around than a compact car and twice as tall. "You live in a town that's celebrating the hundredth anniversary of a vehicular homicide in the name of a pig. Nobody is going to think twice about seeing you in your underwear."

She snorted. "My father is really psyched about the festival this year. Even more so than normal, and he's usually so excited he has a special pair of lucky pajamas he wears for a week straight to celebrate."

Moe had been the mayor of Flat Falls for at least twenty years, and every year his excitement grew. "History…" he'd say in a booming voice to open his festival kick-off speech at the elementary school each spring. "History is what links us together. And Flat Falls is a town with a richer history than most."

He was right. But what they didn't tell us in elementary school was that our quaint little town wasn't founded as the result of a romantic dream for freedom and a better life. Instead, Flat Falls made it onto the map thanks to a Prohibition-era bootlegger turf war gone wrong.

It started with Amos and William Parrish, two brothers in Big River who had nothing better to do than argue with each other, run whiskey, and thumb their noses at local law enforcement. They were both in love with the same woman, a voluptuous redhead named Clara.

Legend has it that one fine May evening, they were fighting over a Model T pickup filled with an order of contraband moonshine and Amos's prized hog, a giant porker named Earl. They were too busy squabbling to notice the Prohibition agents blocking the rickety bridge between the mainland and the small island that housed the boats that would carry their hooch downriver.

Instead of letting himself get arrested, Willy lit the truck on fire and dove into the murky water, leaving his brother to watch the unfortunate demise of both their profits and the pig.

Amos convinced lawmakers that his brother was the mastermind, and two days later, he got revenge for his crispy pig by running over his brother on the side of a deserted country road. Willy lost a leg, and Amos got booted out of town. Their crimson-haired dream girl knew a good opportunity when she saw one and went on to become one of the most infamous rum-runners in North Carolina history.

The two brothers never spoke again, and their feud fueled a hundred-year rivalry between Big River and Flat

Falls. Nothing had been able to bring the two towns together.

Until now.

In less than two weeks, Ruby Fowler, beloved daughter of Flat Falls, was set to marry Warren Levi, the son of a well-known restaurateur from Big River, in the biggest spectacle this town had seen in a hundred years.

I glanced over at the bride-to-be, who was still hunched down in my passenger seat staring wide-eyed at the crowd gathered in front of an architecturally questionable Ferris wheel that had been erected at the edge of a parking lot near the town docks. "Weddings are stressful in the best of circumstances. I imagine it's difficult to do it in the middle of so much…"

"Absurdity?" Ruby supplied.

"I was going to say enthusiasm."

"That, too." Ruby rolled her eyes and brushed a leaf off her thigh. "My father is having a great time reminding me that not only am I getting married, but I'll also be uniting the two kingdoms."

"That's a lot to carry on your shoulders. How does Warren feel about it?"

"That's the problem. I've been so busy that the nerves didn't hit me until today when I saw all the people." She smacked her hands on the dashboard. "But I can't talk to Warren because he's heading offshore with his buddies this afternoon, so he'll be too busy drinking beer and making up stories about the fish he isn't catching to discuss our wedding or the chaos leading up to it."

"Is it his bachelor party?" I asked gently.

"He called me during the fitting to tell me he had made a few last-minute plans. *Last-minute plans*," she repeated, her voice rising. "My bridal luncheon is in two days, and the whole town is invited. He doesn't just get to skip town to play captain with a ship full of mermaids and then show up at the last minute for the ceremony."

I wanted to reassure her, but she was probably right. Warren was a party guy, and even if he'd decided to change for his bride, he was sure to send his bachelor days off with a bang. Or at least a party boat overflowing with half-naked strippers.

On a good day, I couldn't picture him getting excited about spending the afternoon at a glorified bridal shower while the mayor pranced around shaking hands and bartering for votes.

Ruby hopped out onto the sidewalk, her hands fisted. "I can't do this. If he's going to miss the luncheon, I might have to *miss* the wedding."

As I hurried after Ruby, unsuccessfully shielding her body with junk mail from my floorboard, my mind reeled. First, I'd had to track down a missing bride and now I needed to locate an absentee groom.

THE DOORBELL CHIMED as I pushed through to the lobby of Carolina Weddings. Beverlee peered up from behind the reception desk with a lifted brow.

She smacked a bubble of pink chewing gum and trailed a gaze over Ruby, who had the newspaper's coupon section pressed to her chest and was shifting back and forth on the balls of her bare feet. "It appears somebody has been having a day. Is that a good thing or a bad thing?"

I shook my head slightly, but Beverlee didn't notice.

"Because the last time I ended up in the middle of town in my skivvies, it was definitely a good thing," she continued, popping the bubble on the tip of her nose.

I showed Ruby to the restroom and motioned to my

aunt. "Can you call the bridal shop and have them gather Ruby's things?" I lowered my voice. "And grab the dress from my trunk on the way. They'll need to touch it up before the ceremony."

"What kind of touch up? Is it going to require more than stain remover and a pocket sewing kit? I have one of those in my purse, right next to my lock-picking kit."

I glanced over my shoulder to make sure Ruby was still tucked away in the bathroom. "No, this is going to require more… professional attention. And perhaps a round of mythical chanting or a blow torch."

She winced, and I dropped my keys into her outstretched hand. "Good luck. I have a feeling you're going to need it."

Beverlee jangled the keys between her fingers. "Want a hot dog while I'm out?"

"It's not even eleven o'clock."

"They make one with a fried egg and sausage crumbles," she replied, lifting a shoulder. "It's practically breakfast. And I'll pick one up for Ruby, too. She'll need her strength to deal with all those heathens from Big River."

"Careful. I'm one of those heathens of which you speak."

"Nonsense. You've been in Flat Falls since you were five. The sea breeze has surely blown the stink off you by now."

Beverlee had adopted me as a brokenhearted five-year-old after my parents were run off the Big River bridge by a semi in the middle of date night. Ever since then, she had been trying to persuade me I belonged here.

I leaned forward and rested my elbows on the reception desk while Beverlee gathered her purse, an enormous black leather tote featuring an embroidered chicken riding a motorcycle. "I know the mayor is excited about uniting our towns with this festival and then the wedding, but do you really think it's going to happen? Do you remember the last time somebody tried to do that?"

The high school track coach arranged for both teams to have dinner at Denny's following the county championship but ended up with birdshot in his behind after the Flat Falls pole vaulter accused the Big River high jumper of stealing the ketchup.

Nodding solemnly, Beverlee stared out the window. I waved my hand in front of her face to get her attention.

"Sorry," she replied, fanning herself with a bridal magazine from the counter. "Just thinking about Coach Benedict in those athletic shorts." She gave a mournful sigh. "He never did walk right again after that incident, though. Such a shame. It was a difficult time for all of us here in Flat Falls. That was a gold medal tush."

I contemplated smacking my forehead on the counter to rid myself of the image of seventy-five-year-old Bob Benedict ever inspiring female sighs like the one that had just come from my aunt's mouth. The last time I saw him, he was locking me in detention for trying to sneak out the window so I didn't have to spend my Saturday in a classroom that smelled like sweaty feet.

Fortunately, Ruby chose that moment to emerge from the bathroom wrapped in a bright yellow rain jacket that had been abandoned on a hook behind the door. A regretful smile tugged at her lips. "Thanks for talking me down on the bridge."

I gave her a dismissive wave. "Think nothing of it. You're getting married. It would be strange if you didn't spend the next week riding an emotional roller coaster and wanting to kill half the people on your guest list."

"Speaking of which," Beverlee interjected. "Did your mama ever get a response from Warren's family about how they'd like to be seated at the luncheon?"

Ruby's mom had been reaching across the proverbial aisle for weeks now, trying to convince the groom's family to "blend up" the Big River guests with those from Flat Falls, but every time Totty Fowler asked about it, the Levis shot her down.

Ruby shook her head. "She's still working on it."

Which, in Totty-speak, meant she was baking loaves of bread that resembled concrete pavers and delivering geraniums to their front porch with handwritten notes on her monogrammed stationery. She wouldn't give up on her Southern hospitality, even if Virginia Levi knocked her out on the lawn with her own brick of bread.

Ruby's mother took her job as a politician's wife seriously, but she had a history of poor execution. She once tripped over a potted plant during one of Moe's press conferences and took out an entire processional of foreign dignitaries. They landed like dominoes in the hotel fountain, and none of the news reporters caught the mayor's speech because they were too busy filming the mayhem.

Beverlee patted Ruby on the hand. "Bless her heart. Your parents aren't going to give up until every man, woman, child, and stray dog on this coast is holding hands and belting out Kumbaya."

"That's what I'm afraid of," Ruby replied, slumping against the doorframe.

"If they're going to use you to smooth over a hundred years of feuding, you might as well make the best of it," I advised. "So stick your chin up and get ready for battle. You're going to get tomatoes thrown at you from both sides."

"And you'll want to make the best of those tomatoes. We're stopping for hot dogs on the way to the salon. Want to join us?"

"I don't think so," Ruby said with a forlorn glance at the

gown Beverlee had tucked under her arm. "Virginia already warned me that if I ate anything else, I wouldn't be able to fit into my dress."

Beverlee wrinkled her nose. "No bride should have to starve before her wedding day. Next time you design a wedding gown, you should incorporate an elastic waist. And until then, tell your future mother-in-law to mind her own business."

~

ONE ADVANTAGE of living and working in downtown Flat Falls was my proximity to the waterfront. I had easy access to the walking paths and restaurants, and sitting on the swings in front of the Intracoastal Waterway had become my favorite way to unwind after a long day at Carolina Weddings.

During the Roadkill Jubilee, though, the area was crowded with tourists and loud with the sounds of activity. From the backup beeps of trucks delivering supplies to the squeals of kids eating ice cream and playing carnival games, the noise was unrelenting.

I eyed a candy cart parked mere feet from the pawnshop's front door and inhaled the sweet scent of caramel-coated popcorn. I was digging in my purse for a few dollars to grab a bag when shouts erupted from behind the tent that housed the festival's annual barbecue competition.

"I can't believe you forgot the white pepper," a man roared. "Get in your car and go get it. You know they don't carry such things at the Food Barn in Flat Falls."

When the storm of frenzied voices and clashing pans stopped briefly, Beverlee and I studied the tent, anticipating the continued tantrum with enthusiasm we usually reserved for red carpet events or television shows about unhappy housewives.

We weren't disappointed. Within moments, the sound of glass shattering filled the air as the man continued.

"Do I look like I'm kidding?" he bellowed. "You're fired."

A young woman rushed out of the tent, her shoulders slumped and tears streaming down her flushed cheeks.

Ruby ducked her head. "That's my cue," she said, tugging her wedding gown away from Beverlee and scurrying down the street toward the bridal shop.

Beverlee and I tried to sidestep the commotion, but the tent's flap smacked open before we could get away. A giant man emerged from the tent brandishing a set of long metal tongs. He waved them slowly in the air like some sort of culinary divining rod and scanned the small crowd until his eyes rested on me.

He lowered the tongs toward me. "You. Get me some white pepper. And I want the Sarawak variety. Don't you dare come at me with that Indonesian stuff. I'll spit it right in your face."

Surely he wasn't talking to me. My body wouldn't move, but my gaze panned the area to find whatever lowly restaurant worker had been tasked with assisting this man.

His focused glare never left me, though. Instead, he stalked forward and clanged his tongs on the metal light pole next to my head, the sound echoing through the street and drawing curious glances from passersby. "What is it about the women in this town? Are you all stupid?" he asked with a dramatic sigh. "Yes, I'm talking to you."

He leaned in so close I could smell the faint tang of vinegar on his breath. "You. Need. To. Bring. Me. Pepper."

"And you need to back off, Burton," Beverlee ordered as

she hip-checked me out of the chef's long-tonged reach. "Don't you have your own people to terrify?"

I recognized the name immediately. Burton Levi, Big River's closest thing to a celebrity chef and Ruby Fowler's future father-in-law. I hadn't met him yet, because he left the wedding planning to his wife, Virginia.

His temper was legendary, but rumor had it that his seafood bisque was, too. His waterfront Big River restaurant, Lavish, had Michelin stars and a three-month waiting list.

He was larger than life, with a booming voice and a scowl to match. His blond hair stood at attention in starched tufts; even it was afraid to let its guard down around him. His pressed black chef's coat didn't dare display a crumb. It probably repelled stains the same way his personality repelled people.

Beverlee wrapped her fingers around his tongs and yanked them toward her. Burton stumbled, catching himself seconds before he tumbled into the street. "You listen here," she warned. "I'm not sure how you folks talk to each other in Big River, but that's not how we do it around here."

"Stay out of it, Beverlee," he said with a growl, his clean-shaven cheeks reddening as he took me in. "I just need this girl to get me some pepper."

"That girl," Beverlee said, "is my niece, Glory Wells. And she is your son's wedding planner. So I would suggest that unless you want your boy's big day to fall apart like that so-called pumpkin soufflé you serve at your restaurant, you might want to treat her with a bit more respect."

She slapped a twenty-dollar bill on top of the food cart, snatched a bag of pink cotton candy, and motioned for me to follow her down the street.

I peeked back over my shoulder to see my groom's

father seething, his eyes narrowed and fists clenched at his side.

My flip-flops smacked the pavement as I hustled to keep up with Beverlee. "Should you be antagonizing the groom's father like that? His restaurant is a festival sponsor. I'm sure the mayor…"

"The mayor knows what a blowhard Burton is," Beverlee replied. "Those two have known each other since high school."

"So why is there such a push for unity between Big River and Flat Falls if everybody hates each other?"

She halted and turned to me with a smirk. "There are only two reasons people fight wars, Glory. And people end them for the same two reasons."

She stuck one finger up in the air, her sparkling silver nail polish catching the late morning sun's reflection like a piece of aluminum foil. "The first is money."

"And the second?" I asked.

Beverlee adjusted her cleavage and flashed me a saucy grin. "Women."

I looked back over my shoulder, noting that Burton was gone. He must have retreated into his tent, hopefully to find someone on his payroll who could fetch him the pepper before his head exploded. "So, which is it this time?"

Her brows dipped for a moment before she lifted her shoulder in a shrug. "I suspect that it's both."

2

———

The waterfront was bustling with festival preparations by the time Beverlee and I made it to the middle of the town square. We dodged minivans stuffed with pink unicorn pool floats and packs of college girls, their straw bags overflowing with sunscreen and romance novels. Carnival games whirred and buzzed, and the lines for each of the food vendors wound halfway down the waterfront.

I motioned to the hot dog stand. With its shiny silver exterior and the sandwich boards featuring vintage-style illustrations, it had drawn a sizable crowd. "Want to get in line?"

But Beverlee was already surveying the other options. Normally, she was all about sizable crowds. The more people she encountered, the happier she was—unless they were waiting in a line in front of her. If they stood between her and a snack, she'd just as easily toss them into the water as make small talk with them.

"There's ice cream," I suggested, pointing to the frothy pink ice cream van with a bubble machine on its roof.

But her attention was already focused on a rusted truck that sat on a slant at the far end of the parking lot.

Where the other food trucks were vibrant and welcoming, boasting colorful signs that attracted long lines, this one was missing its front bumper, and it was clear, even from across the lot, that its front headlights were dangling near the ground. The bottom half of the truck's body was spray-painted a matte black, and the side wall displayed a slanted decal of three faded bacon slices that looked like earthworms with a skin condition.

Above a torn awning, the words *Big Bacon* were flaking off in petulant sheets, and not a single customer waited outside.

I released a deep sigh. Beverlee had found the outcast.

And I knew before she even made a move that we wouldn't be having ice cream for breakfast. Instead, we'd be ordering from a truck that made me question the last time I had a tetanus shot.

I grabbed her arm and tugged her back. "I don't have time for food poisoning."

"They don't have any customers, Glory. That must feel terrible." She brushed me aside. "And it's just bacon. Have you ever met a bad piece of bacon?"

I squinted at the sign, noting the discoloration from the truck's previous life as a laundry delivery vehicle. Now, it provided breakfast meats instead of starched collars.

She turned back to me with a grin. "Sounds good, doesn't it?"

She race-walked across the parking lot and came to a stop before the truck's open window. When nobody arrived to serve her, she craned her neck and tried to peek inside. "The keys are in there, but it looks abandoned. There are spider webs above the grill."

I shuddered. "It's not too late to wait for a hot dog."

Beverlee ignored me and knocked on the metal. "Hello? Anyone here?"

Moments later, a woman rounded the back of the truck. She wore a dark gray jumpsuit streaked with grease and heavy steel-toed boots, which combined with her scowl made her look like she was either in the middle of doing engine maintenance or taking a break from a work-release program. Her dark hair was cropped in the front, but the back hung in choppy layers that reached her shoulders like it had been styled by a blender. When she saw Beverlee standing at the counter, more eager than a Labrador retriever, her eyes widened in surprise. "Can I help you?"

Beverlee smoothed the front of her pants. "Are you the proprietress of this truck?"

The woman's mouth dipped down into a frown, and she eyed us suspiciously. "Are you from the health department?" She had a thick accent and even thicker biceps, and I wasn't in a hurry to get on her bad side. But before I could ask what she was hiding beneath the griddle that would make a health inspector visit a bad thing, Beverlee stepped toward the drop-down counter and lifted a finger at the faded menu. "Heavens, no. I'm from Flat Falls, and I'd like two orders of bacon, extra crispy. And throw in some tater tots, too."

The chef stared at her for a moment and finally acknowledged her order with a grunt. Apparently satisfied that the white-haired woman in capri pants standing before her ordering meat wasn't a government spy, she dipped her chin and got to work.

While the fryer hissed in the background, Beverlee gave me a satisfied smile. "I always love the first day of the Road-kill Jubilee, don't you?"

Not exactly. Over the years, I had thrown more than my fair share of foul-mouthed teenage fits whenever

Beverlee asked me to do anything remotely family-oriented, especially attending the festival. Or going out in public.

My gaze followed a little girl with shiny brown pigtails as she chased a seagull who had stolen one of her fries. "It was always hard for me. All these happy families."

"That's why this year is so important," Beverlee said, rolling a napkin around a plastic fork. "It's a chance for you to put your bad feelings behind you. A chance for you to help your hometown get a fresh start."

I squeezed her hand, swallowing the lump in my throat. "I got over that years ago, Beverlee."

"Did you?" she asked, a knowing look flitting across her face.

"Yes," I assured her. "I don't resent people just because they're from Big River."

"Even the ones who didn't offer to take you in after your parents died?" she asked, her voice barely a whisper. "That kind of grudge might be worth holding onto."

I didn't have to respond, because a loud shriek jerked our attention toward the front of the bridal shop half a block away.

I whirled around to find Ruby standing in front of the display window, stomping her foot as she held her phone screen out at arm's length.

"At least she has on clothes this time," I noted as Beverlee gathered our orders of bacon from the takeout counter.

Ruby stomped toward us. "He's not answering his phone. He knows I'm upset with him, and he's completely ignoring me."

"Maybe he just doesn't have a good signal," Beverlee suggested.

Beverlee was always the first person to excuse a man for

his poor behavior, but she was also the first in line to string him up when he wronged her more than once.

Ruby waved her phone toward the bridal shop. "His signal would be just fine if he had shown up like he was supposed to. Now I don't even have a ride home, and I'm stuck here in the middle of the festival until my father can pull himself away from the funhouse."

I patted her on the shoulder. "No worries. I wouldn't leave you down here. I'm happy to give you a ride."

Beverlee popped a piece of bacon into her mouth and then offered one to Ruby. "Do they think they'll be able to fix your dress?"

"She said they'd try. If nothing else, I'll just sew on a lace overlay and pretend the dirt underneath was intentional."

"There we go!" Beverlee exclaimed. "It's all going to work out."

"Want me to drop you back at the shop before I take Ruby home?" I asked her.

She shook her head. "No, I'm going to finish my breakfast and then I'll check out the enchilada stand near the waterfront. I hear they have fried oyster tacos, and I want to try them before they sell out."

Beverlee experienced life through her taste buds, but my stomach turned. Even though I grew up on North Carolina seafood, I drew the line at tacos made from seawater-flavored rubber cement. "I'll pass," I replied.

"Are you sure?" she asked, wiggling her eyebrows. "I hear they're a natural aphrodisiac."

"It's not even lunchtime." I gave her a gentle shove. "I don't need an aphrodisiac."

"Oh, to be young again," she said with a wistful sigh. Tossing a wave over her shoulder, she pushed through the crowd toward the waterfront.

I stifled a laugh with the back of my hand. "Sorry about Beverlee. She gets a little too enthusiastic sometimes."

"Are you kidding me?" Ruby asked. "She's the woman I dreamed of being when I was in cotillion class in high school."

I unlocked my passenger door, wincing as it creaked loudly. "Hop in."

She slid into the passenger seat with a smile, folding her hands in her lap. "Thanks. I really appreciate not having to bother my dad. He's under a lot of pressure trying to figure out how to bring in enough tourism dollars to keep the business owners down here happy. No money equals no votes, and the last few years have been rough. My mom said he has been so stressed that he can't sleep, so he prowls around at night eating chips and keeping her up. She finally made him a snack basket and sent him to the guest room."

I backed the car into traffic, carefully avoiding the steady stream of people winding their way down toward the water. "He should be pleased, then. It looks like the festival is going to have quite a turnout this year."

I glanced at a family making their way down the sidewalk and fought a pang of memories as the couple swung the child between them high into the air. The little girl's squeals flitted through my open window, and my chest tightened.

Most of the memories I had of my parents centered around this festival. My mind whirled with flashes of playing carnival games and eating fried dough with our feet dangling over the seawall. I remember bright colors and bold laughter, my parents' love for each other and for me permeating every wisp of memory.

Even after their accident, Beverlee would bring me down here on the first Friday of the festival every year, hoping to keep the tradition alive. School let out early, and a wave of high-energy kids flooded the streets to play games and eat junk food.

As I got older, I'd tell her I didn't want to come, that the festival was for babies, and she'd pat me on the cheek and drag me down here anyway.

"My father invited the whole town to the bridal luncheon," Ruby said, pointing to a parking lot blocked off with orange traffic barrels. "And he ordered a party tent that's big enough to cover the entire lot."

"I know. The party supply company had to order a new one. Moe said the tents they had on hand weren't nearly large enough to house the kind of celebration that would join Flat Falls and Big River." I smiled. "Oh, and his daughter and her new husband."

She chuckled. I slowed down behind a line of traffic that was waiting for an alpaca to cross the street toward the petting zoo.

"Bet you never thought you'd share a wedding venue with farm animals."

Ruby sighed. "No, I actually told my parents that Warren and I were going to elope."

I could understand her concern. What had started out as an intimate wedding for Ruby and Warren had turned into a bout of political theater. Moe had insisted on opening up the bridal shower to the entire town as a part of the festivities and calling it a luncheon because he said it sounded fancier and wouldn't make the underprivileged citizens feel forced to show up with a present.

"You're going to love it," the mayor had told us. "And it will be a great way for our family to give back to the residents of Flat Falls who have supported us over the years."

But Moe's appetite for attention was bigger than his budget, so Ruby and I had spent the last few weeks scaling back his overzealous plans into something a little less grand.

We'd gone the do-it-yourself route for favors, canceled the fire dancers, and picked up a calligraphy book from the thrift store so Ruby's mom could finish the invitations.

"The mayor can be really persuasive." I nodded toward the alpaca, who refused to budge from the middle of the road. "And it's nice that you agreed to let him use your wedding as a good faith gesture between our two communities."

Ruby sat forward, the whoosh of air from her lungs audible even over the pandemonium outside. "Warren," she said, her voice a low growl.

I craned my neck to peer through the windshield, trying to catch a glance of Warren's floppy brown hair and the trademark pastel polo shirt that made him look like he was about to go golfing. "Did you see him?"

She didn't respond. Instead, she slowly raised her finger to point out the window.

"Oh, good," I said. "I told you he'd show up."

"We need to follow him."

I motioned to the traffic in front of me. "Sorry, but I can't really go anywhere at the moment. Can't you just call him? His cell phone should be working now."

"He wasn't alone," Ruby said, her breath coming out in fury-induced pants. "He was with... her."

"Who? What are you—"

"Follow him!" Ruby demanded, her palm smacking the dashboard.

Just as I began looking around for a parking space to slide into, I felt the full force of Ruby's weight slam into my right thigh.

The Honda lurched forward, barely missing the minivan sitting feet in front of me. "Ruby, what is wrong with you?" I screamed, trying to wrench the steering wheel away from her white-knuckled grip.

"Go!" she said, her elbow jabbing me in the thigh as she fought me for control.

She leaned down again, forcing my leg onto the gas pedal as she jerked the wheel toward the sidewalk.

Her long hair slapped against my face and wound its way into my mouth. I wanted to slap her hands away, but by this time she was practically sitting in my lap.

The car jumped onto the curb with a loud *thunk*.

I finally shoved Ruby back into the passenger seat and looked up to see onlookers diving out of the way as my beat-up car hurtled across Town Square, straight toward the statue of Big River Earl.

I slammed on the brakes, but not fast enough. We collided into the base of the statue with enough force to rattle my teeth.

The light through the windshield dimmed, and the last thing I saw before the airbag exploded was a giant bronze pig tumbling into the hood of my car.

~

HOLLIS GOODNIGHT, Flat Falls Police Chief, was the first person on the scene. He wrenched the car door open, his face pinched with worry.

"I should have known it was you," he said, his gruff voice a sharp contrast to the concern in his eyes. He reached in and tugged me out, his steady hands warm against the sudden chill that made my whole body shake. "You okay?"

"I'm fine," I replied, sneaking a glance over at Ruby, who was scrambling to gather her purse's contents from the floorboard.

After she dropped a lipstick into the outer pocket and zipped it closed, she leaned over the center console. She shielded her eyes from the sun as she batted her lashes toward Hollis. "Chief, I know you're going to want to talk to me, but do you mind if I run around that corner to grab Warren?" she drawled in a sweet voice. "We've been missing each other this morning, and we've got a lot of planning to do if we're going to make this festival a success."

Before Hollis could speak, I edged in next to him. "We crashed, Ruby. It's against the law to leave the scene of an accident, especially one that you caused."

"I know," she said, holding up a finger. "And I'll explain everything in a minute, after I find out what Warren was doing with that tramp Ella May Wilkerson."

I had the feeling Hollis was about to let her go, but just before he could fall prey to a pretty girl's feminine wiles, a scream shrilled from in front of the car.

I trailed him as he rushed toward the noise, pushing my way through the crowd that had gathered at the base of the statue where Big River Earl once proudly stood.

In the middle of the throng, a young woman balanced atop a pile of rubble with one fist pressed to her mouth. Her other hand gripped the slab of broken concrete that stretched six feet wide across the base of the statue, her knuckles whitening in protest.

"Ma'am, are you okay?" Hollis asked, gingerly approaching her with his palms out until she stopped screaming. "I know it was a frightening noise, but both passengers are fine. I'm sure there's a perfectly reasonable explanation for why Miss Wells here was taking a joyride on the sidewalk in the middle of the festival."

I shot Hollis a glare and noticed the woman's trembling finger pointing toward the cavity in the base of the statue. In the center of a hollowed-out depression rested a life-sized skeleton wrapped in a vintage biker jacket.

Even though the last year had led to me encountering more than my fair share of freshly dead bodies, I had never seen an actual skeleton. Mrs. Upchurch, my high school anatomy teacher, kept a plastic replica of one on a stand next to her chalkboard, but he didn't count. She called him Albert and dressed him in costume for every major holiday. He was like our class pet, but he didn't chew up the furniture or have accidents on the floor.

This wasn't Albert.

Leaning in closer, I tried to make sense of the pile of bones and the remnants of black leather and tattered denim. I'm not sure what I expected a skeleton to look like, but I didn't think it would be dressed like a greaser sporting a knobby, skull-shaped ring that bore a striking resemblance to the man's actual head. I turned toward Hollis with wide eyes.

But he was already ushering the bystanders away and speaking into the radio nestled in his belt. "I'm going to need a crime scene team down here at the statue," he said in a low voice and turned to meet my curious gaze. "It looks like Glory has found another body."

3

———

After Hollis questioned me for far longer than necessary about how my Honda had ended up wearing the town's mascot, I walked back to Carolina Weddings.

As soon as I opened the door, Beverlee jumped up from behind the desk and rushed forward to engulf me in a tight hug. "Scoots just texted me about what happened. Did you really end up with Big River Earl as your new hood ornament?"

Scoots Gillespie ran the pawnshop down near the waterfront and had made it her life's work to be smack dab in the middle of all Flat Falls gossip. Since she was also Beverlee's best friend, the news of my accident probably made it across town faster than if the whole incident had been live-streamed on YouTube.

"Did Scoots also mention the surprise that was hidden underneath the statue?"

"You mean Rocky Boyd's body?"

I stepped backward and stumbled into the door. "Rocky

Boyd?" I repeated. "As in my father's brother? The one who ran away from town after my parents died?"

"That's the one," Beverlee answered with a curt nod. "Scoots recognized him from the leather jacket and that oversized skull ring he used to wear." She shook her head. "Should have known he didn't disappear like everybody said. It's just like him to have been hanging out in the middle of Flat Falls this whole time. He has probably been cursing every single one of us from his prized perch in the great beyond."

"He's dead, Beverlee," I said, stepping around her and dropping my purse behind the desk. "It's not like he made a choice to go belly-up under a giant oxidized pig and then spent the next few decades haunting the neighborhood out of spite."

"You never knew your uncle," Beverlee scoffed. "If anybody was going to run a decades-long scam on this entire town, it would have been Rocky Boyd. That man was trouble with a capital letter, and if there was a fight to be had within a thirty-mile radius, you'd better believe he was right in the middle of it."

I hadn't spent much time learning about my father's family. What I did know, I had pieced together from a Google search and a few failed attempts to reach out to my grandmother, a grumpy old woman who had been as interested in raising me as having a colonoscopy for fun.

Beverlee hadn't spoken about them much over the years, either. She'd talk about my parents until her voice went hoarse, but if I asked about my remaining family on the other side of the bridge, she'd respond with muted curses and a quick subject change.

This time, she tried to distract me with scooping birdseed into glassine paper pouches so the guests would have something to toss at Ruby and Warren after the lovebirds said, "I do." The job kept my hands busy, but after about an hour of listening to Beverlee babble about the drapery change they'd made at the senior center, I couldn't hold in my questions any longer.

"I knew my father had a brother, but I've never heard you talk about him much," I said. "Were they close?"

She put down the birdseed bag and stared out the window. I was about to give up on getting a response when she finally spoke. "Daniel and Rocky Boyd were about as different as two people can get," she said, her voice slow and measured. "And their relationship was like a powder keg. It didn't take much for them to explode. Their fights were legendary."

I thought back to my father and his infectious enthusiasm. I remembered his laugh, the way his arm looped around my mother's shoulder whenever we'd walk through the neighborhood and how he'd tweak my nose just before he tucked me in at night. He was a gentle giant with a quick smile, not a brawler intent on pounding his brother into the ground.

My fingers tugged at a thread that had come loose from my sleeve. "That's not how I remember him."

"Your mama kept an ice pack in the freezer specifically for Daniel's black eyes," she said, turning back to study me. "She never could understand how such a good man came from such a bad place."

I gaped at her. "Come on. I know we've all complained about the people in Big River for years, but not everybody that lives across the bridge is a criminal. They're probably all normal people, just like us."

At that moment, Burton Levi crashed through the door and slammed it so hard behind him that the welcome bells flew off and skidded across the floor.

Beverlee walked over and plucked them up, then

smirked at me. "You were saying?"

I shouldered past her and pasted on my sweetest smile. "Mr. Levi, what can I help you with? I trust you found that pepper you were looking for earlier."

He met my greeting with a sharp glare and pounded his fist on the wooden desk. "This is all your fault, and your entire family is going to pay."

My heart lurched, and I debated calling Hollis. In my experience, angry fathers-of-the-groom occasionally required outside intervention. And sometimes handcuffs. But Hollis was no doubt busy with his new friend, Rocky Boyd, so I chose to handle the situation myself.

I glanced over at Beverlee, who was fishing into the basket of cutlery we kept on the sideboard when we had tastings. I wasn't sure what she was planning on doing with the clear plastic spoon she shoved up her sleeve, but it wasn't a match for the big man standing before us.

I motioned for her to stand down before turning back to Burton. "I'm not sure I understand, Mr. Levi. Are you unhappy about the wedding plans?"

He looked confused for a moment before charging forward again. "This isn't about the wedding. This is about a friend I thought was living it up on some foreign island surrounded by beautiful women in bikinis, but instead spent the last twenty-five years stuffed inside an oversized statue in the middle of this backwoods town."

"I didn't know him, but I'm sorry to hear that he passed away," I replied. "It's never easy to lose someone you care about."

"Rocky Boyd was my best friend." His booming voice rattled everything from my stomach to the delicate floral wind chime that hung next to the window. "And he didn't *pass away*. Your father killed him."

I whipped my head around so fast that the room

wobbled. "My father… what?"

Surely he wasn't serious. My father had been gone for twenty-five years. The idea that he was somehow responsible for anyone's death—much less his brother's—was outrageous.

Fury curled inside me and forced my hands into fists. I hadn't gotten into a fight since I was sixteen and a Senior with over-sprayed bangs and an armful of jelly bracelets had jumped me in the bathroom because she caught her boyfriend making eyes at me across the cafeteria.

This time, I wanted to fight.

I wanted to pound my fists into Burton Levi's smug face and demand that he take it back.

But I couldn't, because by the time the room stopped spinning and the haze of anger diminished, Burton Levi had pushed his way back out the door and disappeared into the crowd.

I SLIPPED AWAY from the chaos of downtown later that afternoon to grab some lunch at Trolls. As soon as I pushed open the door, I was met with the smell of hush puppies and Old Bay.

I dropped onto a bar stool, the weight of Burton's accusations sitting on my chest like a sack of wet sand. Nothing ruined a craving for chicken wings faster than a gasbag emboldened by a docket of lies. But even though I knew my father hadn't committed murder, Burton's claims had shined a flashlight into the mom-and-dad-sized hole that I had carried around with me for the last twenty-five years, since that fateful night when they had gone out on a date and never returned.

Ian Strickland, the owner of the restaurant and a long-time friend, cleaned the other end of the bar, chatting with a tourist about the festival. His surfer-blond hair flopped over his forehead while he talked, and he would occasionally brush it away with the back of his hand. When he noticed me, the white cotton towel he was using to scrub the counter came to a stop, his forearms flexing. He studied me for a moment before excusing himself from the conversation and heading toward my end of the bar.

"Rough day?" he asked with a sympathetic smile. He reached a hand under the bar and grabbed a sparkling water, topping it off with a lime wedge.

"How can you tell?" I clasped my fingers around the bottle.

"Besides years of experience?" he said, nodding toward the kitchen. "You usually order food on the way in. My line cooks actually fight over who's going to make your nachos, but they're just standing around looking lonely and not cooking."

My stomach rebounded from its pout and let out an impertinent growl. I followed his gaze and gave the two chefs standing expectantly at the kitchen door a quick wave.

"So if you're not here for food, you must be here for something else."

"Can't a girl come in to see one of her oldest friends without having an ulterior motive?"

"Sure," he replied, retrieving a basket of crackers from under the counter. He pushed it across the bar toward me. "But not when that girl is you."

He knew me well. I had been pulling that trick on him since we were teens making out underneath the bleachers during high school football games. I flattened my hand on the bar and let out a dramatic sigh. "Fine. I've had a terrible morning, and I came in here to get away from it. But then you mentioned nachos, and now I want to eat my feelings."

He grinned and gestured to the cooks, who scrambled back into the kitchen.

"I also wanted to follow up on the food for the bridal luncheon. Are you sure you ordered enough shrimp?"

"Of course," he responded with a brisk nod, drawing his phone out of his back pocket and scrolling through the screen. "I called the guy with the white panel van who sometimes parks out at the docks. He assured me his second cousin is a fisherman who can get us a good deal on the shrimp that none of the other restaurants wanted to buy. Overstock, if you will. He'll just back right on up to the table and dump them out. A week from Tuesday, right?"

Panic swirled low in my belly. The mayor had entrusted me with planning a classy celebration. A random guy with an unrefrigerated van and a pile of seafood scraps wasn't going to cut it, especially if he showed up on the wrong day. "No, that's not right…"

He only let me suffer for a moment before he tossed the bar cloth into a dishpan behind him and spun toward me, the dimple flashing in his cheek. "Relax, Glory. It's not my first catering job. Everything's under control."

I pressed my hand to my chest. "Not funny, Ian."

"It was a little funny. I've never seen those big brown eyes look so terrified. Not even after you've found a dead body."

I groaned and rolled my shoulders, then downed a long sip from the bottle of water. "Don't remind me. I seem to have a knack for uncovering corpses these days."

"I heard. What do you have against that statue, anyway?"

This hadn't been my first run-in with Big River Earl. I once took out his left femur with Beverlee's fender when I spilled a milkshake in my lap trying to keep Joey Ripple from getting handsy. The town held an emergency meeting and ended up using money they had reserved for replacing the carpet in the elementary school library to commission a new statue.

As far as I could tell, they had never replaced the carpet, which explains why the librarian shot daggers out of her eyes whenever she saw me at the Grind and Go. That, or the fact that I used to skip PE and read *Cosmo* in the study carrels because I hated running laps.

"It wasn't my fault," I said. "Ruby is convinced there's some sort of hanky-panky going on between Warren and a girl from the mainland. He isn't returning her calls, and he showed up in town with a mysterious brunette on his arm. Ruby went a little crazy on my gas pedal leg, and the next thing I knew, Big River Earl was taking a nosedive toward my windshield."

Ian grimaced. "Sorry about your Honda."

"She was a good car. She deserved to go down in a blaze of glory instead of humiliation." I waved my hand in the air. "I haven't really had time to process it. Right after it happened, Burton came in and accused my father of murder. The jerk."

"Burton Levi?" he asked, a furrow settling between his brows.

"You know him?"

Ian practically growled. "Know him? I worked for him at Lavish after you left. Worst two years of my life."

"I didn't know you worked in Big River."

He lifted a brow. "If I remember correctly, you were busy marrying another man."

"Touché." Ian was right, though. I had bolted from Flat Falls—and him—immediately after high school, but instead of the sparkling city life I imagined, I wound up marrying a crook who stole both my savings and my dignity. I took another long draw from the bottle. Wanting to change the subject as quickly as possible, I added, "Was Burton always a tyrant?"

"Tyrant's a bit of an understatement. I was always surprised he didn't rupture his vocal cords from yelling all the time."

"What finally made you quit?"

"He fired me. Right after he threw a five-hundred-dollar bottle of chianti at my head and tried to disintegrate my apron with a kitchen torch."

"Ouch."

"But it turned out to be a good thing." Ian gestured around the bar. "If he hadn't lost his marbles that night, I doubt I would have ended up here."

"I'm glad there's no bad blood between you. I'd hate for there to be a fistfight at the bridal luncheon. Blood stains would be hard to conceal on the linens."

"I never said there weren't bad feelings. Just because he pushed me into opening my own place doesn't mean I'd be opposed to stabbing him in the temple with a fork if the opportunity presented itself."

"Noted," I said, glancing up to see Moe Fowler pushing his way through the restaurant's door.

The mayor's cheeks were flushed, and he fanned himself twice with a folded-up newspaper before approaching us.

He slipped off his khaki fisherman's hat and smacked it on the bar. Moe wanted people to think it was for sun protection, but everybody knew he wore it to hide the growing bald spot on his head.

We'd all watched with sympathetic amusement over the years as he'd experimented with hair pieces and comb-over techniques. He once let the owner of the party supply store talk him into a wig, and when it kept slipping over his eyes during city council meetings, he'd glued it to his scalp.

Unfortunately, he used Superglue, and he'd been stuck with a mullet for weeks.

I spotted a brown smear on the hat's rim. Evidently, he'd been using root cover-up spray again, hoping nobody would notice that he'd spray-painted his scalp. Paint wouldn't even stick to the buildings in the Carolina humidity, and I doubted he'd have any better luck getting it to adhere to his shiny pate.

I covered my mouth so a snicker couldn't escape.

Ian rescued me from certain embarrassment. "Mayor Fowler, you've been doing an outstanding job with the festival, as always. Just let us know if there's anything you need. I'm sure the citizens of Flat Falls will step up to help you in any way we can."

"That's actually why I'm here." Moe preened a bit before clearing his throat. "We've got a bit of a problem—not with the festival, of course, but with the wedding preparations."

I sat up straighter on my stool. "What kind of problem?"

He shifted his glance around the room, presumably to ensure that no errant Big River spies were lurking in a corner eating steak fries. "It's about your uncle."

A quick burst of memory reminded me of the leather-wearing corpse I uncovered with my car that morning, and my molars scraped against each other before I was able to speak again. "They haven't proved that the body under that statue was Rocky Boyd."

With a look of undisguised impatience, Moe let out a snort. "We all know who that leather jacket and skull ring belonged to, Glory."

I waved my hand in the air. "Fine, even if it was my long-lost uncle from Big River underneath the pig, what does that have to do with the wedding?"

He leveled me with an annoyed gaze and fiddled with

the brim of his hat. "Burton wants to cancel it."

"The wedding?"

Moe nodded, his puffy lower lids drooping even further than normal. "The whole point of having the wedding during the festival was to bring our two towns together."

I frowned. I thought the whole point was to get his daughter married.

"But they can't get married because there was a dead guy that nobody even liked stuffed under a statue for who knows how long?" I asked.

"Exactly. Burton is threatening to go to the press about your father." He flattened his hand against the bar.

Rage bubbled up from low in my belly, but before I could respond, Ian tapped his index finger on the bar. "Wait a second. What does Glory's dad have to do with this? He died twenty-five years ago."

Moe's frown matched mine. "Burton is alleging that Daniel killed his brother. And if he goes to the press, the whole festival will collapse. And no festival means no tourism. Nobody wants to eat a corn dog next to a corpse."

I couldn't argue there. "But my father didn't kill Rocky."

"Regardless, we have to keep this whole scandal quiet for the next week. Until after the wedding." Moe shifted on the stool and raked a quivering hand across his scalp before pointing at Ian. "And that's where you come in."

Ian shook his head. "No. I'm not standing in the way of a police investigation."

Moe blinked for a moment and let out an awkward laugh. "Of course not."

"What do you need from him, then?" I asked.

"To cancel the catering contract for Ruby's bridal luncheon," Moe replied quietly. "That's the only thing keeping Burton from taking his theory to the press and ruining the whole festival."

4

————

I was still fuming when Hollis dropped me off in Beverlee's driveway later that afternoon. Since I didn't have a car, he offered me a ride to her house for our regular Wednesday night supper.

I slid out of the passenger seat and lingered with my arm on top of the door. I gazed at the laptop and stacks of paper he had shoved aside for me to climb in the front seat. "Thanks for not making me ride in the back like a criminal."

He gave me a soft smile in return. "The day's still young."

I motioned toward the garden, where Beverlee was sure to be feeding homemade granola to her chickens or devising a plan to woo her next husband with a concoction of herbs and sticks. "Want to come in? I'm sure she would love to see you."

And the feeling would be reciprocated, no doubt. Hollis had been secretly in love with my aunt for as long as I could remember, which usually resulted in him shooting her starry-eyed glances while she flirted with other men and set him up on blind dates with her friends.

Hollis glanced over my shoulder before shaking his head. "As much as I'd like to enjoy this afternoon in the company of two beautiful women, I've got a dead body and a handful of intoxicated tourists to keep me busy."

I thanked him and shut the car door. Beverlee's back gate screeched open as I watched him speed off.

"Was that Hollis?" she asked, craning her neck to peer down the street lined with live oak trees and homey bunga-lows. She was dressed in cutoff jeans and a white eyelet halter top, a wide-brimmed pink sun hat perched on top of her head. "Why didn't he stay? I have lingonberry scones."

My stomach growled. I hadn't eaten anything since that mid-morning bacon snack. "I don't even know what lingonberries are, but I'll take his."

Beverlee motioned for me to follow her through the gate, clucking her tongue as she closed it behind us. Within seconds, my sister-chicken bobbled through the yard.

When I graduated from high school and left Flat Falls, my aunt began opening her home and her kitchen to other orphans. Over the years, that had included a poodle with an eye patch and a turtle who sported a 3D-printed shell from the high school shop class.

Most recently, she had acquired a bunch of chickens from a trailer park that was about to be bulldozed for high-dollar condos. And now Beverlee had Matilda, a feathery diva she doted on with handmade mealworm cookies and chicken pedicures.

She pushed open the sliding glass door from her back patio to the kitchen. The peppy *guggle guggle* Matilda made as she cut me off sounded an awful lot like gloating.

"Matilda is in a good mood today," I remarked. The glossy black chicken pranced around the kitchen waiting for whatever baked good Beverlee was about to bestow upon her.

"She's just excited. Before you got here, I was telling her about how I visited Bernie Ellerman in the hospital yesterday. He broke his hip trying to record himself doing a striptease on TikTok."

I shuddered. "Isn't he in his seventies?"

Beverlee grinned. "Yes, but he's very spry. And he would have made quite the video, except he got his foot caught in the sleeve of his jacket as he was whirling it around the room. He took a nasty tumble and broke his collarbone. Doc Willis said he's not allowed to make any more videos for at least six weeks."

I shook my head, confused. "But what does this have to do with your chicken?"

"Well, they have a program at the hospital where therapy dogs come in and visit all the old people to keep their spirits up, and I had the most wonderful idea."

I knew where this was going. "Let me guess. Therapy chickens?"

"Yes!" she exclaimed, sliding a scone from the cooling rack onto a plate. "Don't you think my girl would be able to cheer people up better than a silly old cocker spaniel?"

I shot a glance at Matilda, who was standing on the kitchen tile next to Beverlee's foot.

When Beverlee gestured toward the table with the plate and offered it to me, I smirked toward the chicken, only slightly mortified that I was competing with poultry for a piece of pastry. I might not have been the first in the door, but at least I was getting scone priority.

But when Beverlee plucked off a corner of her own scone and started blowing on it, I knew I was mistaken. As she deposited the steaming crumble on the floor in front of Matilda, I accepted that, when it came to Beverlee, my humanity wasn't getting me to the front of the attention line.

After she fed Matilda an extra half a scone from her own plate, my aunt turned toward me with a questioning look. "What brings you here this afternoon? I thought your hands were going to be full of wedding preparations for the rest of the day."

I brushed a crumb off the front of my shirt. "I need you to tell me why Burton Levi thinks Dad killed Uncle Rocky."

She pressed her hip against the counter and raised a brow. "Oh, is that all?"

"I'm serious, Beverlee. The mayor took the contract for the bridal luncheon away from Ian because he thinks Burton has something on Dad. Now, all these months of planning have gone to waste, and the whole festival is on the brink of collapse."

She snorted, then slapped her hand across her mouth. "Sorry, that wasn't very ladylike. I was just trying to picture your father killing somebody."

Although my memories of him were fleeting and spotty, I also knew he hadn't done it. He was a good man, a kind man, who had been taken from me way too young. And even if they had proof that he had been an ax murderer who wore nothing but hot pink chaps to decapitate his victims, I wouldn't have believed them. Daniel Boyd was a by-the-book bank manager by day and a teddy bear by night. His world revolved around me and my mother, and until that fateful evening when the truck crashed into them and sent them tumbling over the bridge to Big River, my world had revolved around him, too.

I didn't need crime scene photos or forensic analysis. My gut just knew.

My father was innocent.

Sadness tugged at my chest, and Beverlee reached over and squeezed my hand.

I took a shaky breath. "Tell me everything about my dad and his brother."

Usually, Beverlee adored an invitation to spill her guts. But just like after the accident, she remained eerily quiet.

"Beverlee," I warned. "I know you've spent the last eighteen years protecting me, and I appreciate that—but I'm not a child anymore, and I need to know the truth. There's nobody left to protect my parents but me."

She paused, then dipped her chin once. "Daniel and Rocky were like vinegar and salt water. There have never been two brothers that were more different."

That much I could believe. I didn't have any memories of my uncle, but from what I'd heard over the years, he was a troublemaker, prone to fights and arrested more than once on charges of public intoxication. Rocky Boyd was a rotten seed. My father had done the right thing by steering clear of him.

"Daniel never fit in with the Big River crowd. And when he fell in love with Lucy, it just made sense for them to start their life together here in Flat Falls," she continued. "But Rocky never let him forget where he came from. They came to blows more than once."

"But isn't that just what brothers do? Fight with each other?"

"Not like this," Beverlee said, rising to gather our plates and rinse them off in the sink. "They hated each other with the kind of fury that comes from a lifetime of buildup."

"And what did Grandma have to say about that? I'm sure she didn't want—"

"Ada said that if your father ever came back to Big River, she'd meet him at the town lines with Busy."

"Busy?" I asked.

"Her shotgun."

I could picture it. My left big toe was more maternal than my grandmother. With hair the color of washed-up oyster shells and squinty eyes, Ada Boyd was a walking scowl.

The last time I saw her was on the afternoon of my sixteenth birthday, right after I got my driver's license. I had paced at the DMV, more nervous about going to Big River than I had been to parallel park Beverlee's enormous gold Buick. But it felt like a momentous day, one that I ought to share with the rest of my family.

Even the ones who didn't want me.

I hadn't told Beverlee where I was going, but she let me borrow her car anyway, and I made the drive across the bridge with shaking hands.

My grandmother met me on her dilapidated front porch before I had a chance to knock. "What do you want?" she had asked, her tone gruff and disapproving. She leaned up against the column with one hand on her hip and the other entwined in a dirty floral apron that hung loosely around her waist.

I remember pasting on my friendliest smile. "I'm Glory. Your… granddaughter."

"I know who you are, girl," she said. "I just don't know why you're here."

I didn't know, either. Maybe because I needed a connection with my parents on that milestone birthday. Or maybe because I wanted to know why she hadn't ever answered my letters. I didn't expect to find her refrigerator plastered with photos of my birthday parties taken from afar with a telephoto lens, but I expected her to be pleased to see me.

"It's my birthday," I said, the remnants of my pancake breakfast churning in my stomach. Beverlee had added whipped cream and sprinkles and had brought the tray to my room with blazing candles and an off-key song. "My sixteenth. And I thought we could—"

"You look like your mama," she interrupted with a growl. "Now get off my property."

So I left. And I sat on the side of the bridge soaking Beverlee's upholstery with my mascara-streaked tears until she and Hollis had pulled up, wrapped me in a blanket, and taken me home.

I shook my head, pulling myself back to Beverlee's kitchen table. "I just don't get it, then. Rocky Boyd was a loose cannon who came from a long line of loose cannons. Why does everybody think my father had something to do with him being stuffed into a statue?"

"We never knew what happened to him. He just disappeared the same night your parents died."

"The exact same night?"

She nodded. "Rumor was that he got spooked after the accident and left Big River."

"Why was he spooked?" I asked.

"Because some people in Flat Falls blamed him for your parents' death."

"They died in an accident."

"Yes, but the night Daniel and Lucy died, the brothers had a huge fight. The biggest one I can remember them having. Lots of bad blood passed between them, and there were threats."

"Threats? To my parents?"

"There were threats on both sides. Everybody was wrapped up in the Founder's Day Festival, and those boys came to blows in the middle of the town square. Rocky held a knife to Daniel's throat." Beverlee swallowed, her expression grim. "And then Daniel threatened to kill him in front of the whole darn town."

~

After she fed me, Beverlee drove me back to my apartment above the pawnshop. It was barely seven, but I was ready to curl up on the couch and binge-watch reality television until drool cemented my face to the cushions.

Planning a wedding in the midst of a spectacle had become my specialty, but it was exhausting.

I had just dropped onto the sofa with my phone in one hand and the remote in the other when a knock sounded at my door. With a groan, I called out, "Are you here to tell me I won the lottery?"

The door swung open. Scoots stood at the threshold. She was lit up from behind, the apartment's exterior yellow bug light reflecting off her spiky white hair. She looked larger than her five-foot-two frame would suggest.

"Not the lottery," she said. "Better. I brought you a Mustang."

"You brought me a horse?" I asked.

"Not a horse. A car. And a mighty sexy one, too. A girl like you deserves something better than that bucket of rust and ripped upholstery you used to drive. Not to mention that it smelled like cheese straws and old boots."

Despite being full of bluster, Scoots was one of the most generous people I knew. Even more so when it involved giving away her ex-husband's prized sports car.

My eyes teared up, and I pressed a fist to my chest. "You didn't have to do that."

"Well, I heard you ran your other one into a crowd at the festival, and I had an extra car just sitting around." She dangled the keys in the air. "Aren't you going to invite me in?"

"You own the building. Since when do you require an invitation?"

My apartment was one of two that sat above the only pawnshop in Flat Falls, accessible by a rickety metal staircase in the alley behind the building. My friend Josie, who was finishing up her house arrest sentence for embezzlement, occupied the other apartment.

Scoots tossed the keys on my coffee table before plopping onto the sofa next to me.

As if on cue, Josie appeared in the doorway, a pizza box in hand.

"I heard you ran over a team of nuns who were there to bless the festival," she said, flipping open the pizza and resting the box on the table in front of us. "Figured you might be hungry."

I pegged her with an annoyed glare. "There were no nuns. Nobody got hurt. And besides, it wasn't my fault. Ruby climbed on top of me while I was driving, and she mashed my gas pedal foot."

Scoots turned to me and lifted both a brow and a finger. "One—what was the mayor's daughter doing climbing on top of you while you were driving? That seems like something you should save for non-driving times."

Then she swiveled toward Josie, who had folded herself onto the side chair that flanked the sofa. "And two—what were you thinking, getting pineapple on pizza?" She plucked a piece of pineapple off her slice and inspected it with a wrinkled nose and then threw it back in the pizza box.

I leaned forward and picked up the keys, gaping at them in wonder. "You really brought me a muscle car?"

"Sure. It has been sitting in the garage since I took it from George in the divorce." Scoots sighed. "He loved that car more than he loved me."

I tried to push the keys back into Scoots's hand to no avail. "Thank you, but I can't take it," I said, even though my half-hearted protests were useless. "This car is worth more than I make in a year."

"You need a better car if you're going to go knocking down statues. You want to make a statement, and that old Honda just doesn't say the right things."

"It said I was sensible." I crossed my arms and stuck out my chin.

"Exactly!" Scoots declared. "And nobody wants to look sensible. Now you'll be driving around this fiery beauty. The nuns will jump out of your way when they see you coming in this."

"For the last time, I did not run over any—"

"What's the deal between you and Ruby's new father-in-law?" Josie interrupted. "The pizza delivery guy said he saw the police trying to break up a fight between you."

I pinched the bridge of my nose. There were a lot of things I liked about returning to my hometown. The hyper-active rumor mill was not one of them. "Burton was just upset because it was his best friend under the statue."

"It's crazy that Rocky Boyd has been here the whole time. I thought that guy ran off to join the circus. Or the military." Scoots yanked off another piece of pineapple. "I can't remember. The nineties are a bit of a blur."

"Well, I can assure you there was no circus. Apparently, he just got himself stuck under a pig."

"That's not a very nice thing to say about Burton's wife," Scoots said.

My jaw dropped. "I wasn't... Burton's wife?"

"Sure," Scoots replied. "Rocky was a well-known ladies' man. Everybody knew that a wedding band wasn't enough to make him mind his manners. Supposedly, he and Virginia Levi had been sneaking around behind Burton's back for years. He was a rebel with a fast car and a devil-may-care attitude, and he was like flypaper for the ladies."

I thought about the pictures I had seen of my uncle over the years. Sure, he had thick black hair and a leather jacket, but that was where the bad boy allure ended. He seemed like the type to be doused in cheap gas station cologne, calling everybody "babe."

Or maybe things had just been different back then. A skull ring and a thick gold chain wound through bear-like chest hair could have been a turn-on.

"Burton insists that my father killed Rocky, and I'm not sure how to prove him wrong."

"That's easy," Scoots said, flicking an errant piece of pineapple onto her napkin. "You've got to pay a visit to your grandmother. If anyone has details about what happened between Rocky and Daniel, it's her."

5

―――――――

I drove slowly across the bridge, half expecting a curtain of darkness to slam shut behind me as I passed the rusted *Welcome to Big River* sign. But nothing changed. Huddles of seagulls perched atop the pilings along the waterway, seagrass whipped onto the road in both directions, and the salty breeze felt the same on one side of the bridge as it did on the other.

The isolated stretch of road eventually bloomed into a town, colorful rows of cottages separating it from the beach. Front porches overflowed with flower boxes and vibrant, welcoming flags. Across the street, billboards advertised tourist shops selling hermit crabs, boogie boards, and enormous beach towels. But never once did a horned devil poke his head out from behind a shrub to shoot me down with eye lasers the way people from Flat Falls would have had me believe for all these years.

Big River was just like any other coastal town in Eastern North Carolina.

I slowed down as I passed Burton's restaurant, noting that even though it was only mid-morning, a crowd had formed on the waterfront patio, waiting for his latest culinary masterpiece. The scent from the smoker carried across the street, and I had to admit that even though their chef was a foul-mouthed beast, his food smelled delicious.

But as I turned down a side street a few blocks from the popular waterfront area, the ambiance changed. Where the houses a few streets over were bright with lush greenery and festive Adirondack chairs, this side of town looked like someone had tried to drain out all the color. Cinder block houses streaked with rust from long-neglected flagpoles sat in dejected rows next to the road.

Ada Boyd's house fit right in.

The sidewalk buckled from old tree roots and years of neglect, and the roof drooped in despair under the weight of one too many days in the unrelenting sun. Even the mailbox was gray and crooked.

The only thing colorful was a bit of graffiti on the side of the house that said "Go Away" in dripping red letters. It looked like a killer's calling card. I double-clicked the Mustang's lock before venturing toward the house.

When a black cat hissed from the shadows beneath a scraggly bush, I stumbled, pressing my hand to my chest to stop the thundering of my heart. He bolted across the crunchy brown grass and escaped through a hole in the chain-link fence that leaned over a neighbor's yard.

This is where my father grew up.

I tried hard to picture my daddy, with his boisterous laugh and endless optimism, as a product of this environment. There was so much... gray. I swallowed against the emotions rising in my throat.

The stairs creaked as I inched up to the front door. I clenched the railing, its chipped paint sticking to my palms.

I rapped my knuckles against the wood and attempted to peek through the glass, but crinkled newspaper was taped to the inside of the three rectangular windows near the top of the door. From the paper's yellowed edges and the headline about a hurricane that had torn through the island nearly a decade before, Ada Boyd wasn't fond of redecorating.

I had almost given up and was turning back toward the car when the door creaked open.

"It's you," she observed, her voice gravelly and her brown eyes squinting against the onslaught of daylight.

I swiveled, prepared to greet the woman that I had not seen in fifteen years. I held back a gasp as I took her in. Her thin gray hair wound through light pink curlers that stuck out at odd angles, and she was covered from neck to ankle in a polyester quilted muumuu.

For a moment, I felt guilty for letting all these years pass without at least checking on her. We might not be close, but she was still family. And family always looked out for each other. At least that's what Beverlee insisted every time she asked me to accompany her to poker night with the Methodist Ladies' Book Club.

I swallowed, then raised my hand in greeting. "Hi, Grandma," I said, trying to conceal the wobble in my voice.

"It's about time you got here." She nudged the door open with a bony shoulder and cast a wary glance out over the street. "Now get inside before somebody sees you."

THE INSIDE of my grandmother's house was as nondescript as the outside. It smelled musty and old, like wet books and burnt TV dinners. The furniture blended together in various shades of tan and gold, and the wood paneling held the orange cast of age and smoke.

A lopsided recliner sat in the corner, its stuffing

exploding out around exposed springs, and a brown crocheted blanket was balled into a misshapen lump in the center.

I glanced around and forced a smile. "Your home is lovely."

She snorted, which progressed into an all-out cough. I was afraid her lungs were going to come flying out of her chest and splatter on the faux wood tray that leaned against her stained corduroy sofa.

She finally got control of the hacking and regarded me with an impatient sigh. "Let's not make small talk, girl. You're here for one reason only, and that is to get the information you need to find out who killed my son."

I cast a confused glance around the room, wondering how she had known I was coming before I showed up on her doorstep. My heart thumped, and I stepped toward her, hopeful she was finally open to talking to me about my parents. "My father?"

"No," she replied with a dismissive wave. "Rocky. I heard you ran over a group of kindergarteners during the festival and knocked into the statue. I figured you were here to make amends."

The rumor mill was as exuberant in Big River as it was in Flat Falls. And as misinformed. "There were no kinder—"

She lifted her palm to stop me. "You found his body, now it's up to you to find his killer."

I wasn't sure I followed her logic, but this was the longest conversation I'd ever had with my grandmother, so I wasn't about to give it up.

She didn't wait for me to acknowledge her request. Instead, her pale blue chenille slippers made a scratching sound on the linoleum as she shuffled across the floor toward a closet on the other side of the room. She tugged open the bifold doors, kicking aside a puzzle box and a metal bucket that had clattered to the floor.

"Over here," she said. "I need you to get the box from the top shelf."

I followed her and she pointed up at the shelf. Aside from two cardboard boxes, it was crammed full of photo albums, old records, and a year's supply of cheap toilet paper.

My fingers itched to pull down a photo album and trail through my father's life before he came to Flat Falls, but Ada nudged me with a bony finger and gestured to the box on the right.

"That one's Rocky's. It has everything I could find from the time he disappeared."

"Why don't you give it to the police? They're the ones who solve old murders, not me. I'm just a wedding planner."

"I've heard about you," she said, narrowing her eyes to inspect me. "I heard how you solved all of those other murders. Seems like you're at least partially capable of doing it. And besides, you owe me."

Part of me wanted to argue that I didn't owe her anything. She was the one who abandoned me with Beverlee when I was five years old. But the other part wanted to stay locked inside the house where my father was raised, fingers gripped around that tenuous connection, even if it meant doing so in the presence of someone who didn't want me there.

I carefully tugged the box off the shelf, and a puff of dust tickled my throat.

"Rocky was a good boy," Ada said, nodding once.

"What about my father?" My voice trembling, I glanced at the other box on the shelf. "Do you have anything of his, too?"

She practically growled in response. "I'm not talking to you about Daniel. Not until you figure out who was responsible for sticking my baby underneath that wretched pig."

I tucked the box under my arm. "Some people think Dad might have had something to do with Rocky's death. What do you think?" My stomach turned even as the words left my mouth.

Ada pursed her lips. "I think that's for you to find out." She thumped the box and motioned toward the door. "Now go before anybody sees you."

As I stepped onto the porch, my cheeks flamed in the familiar humiliation of her rebuffs. I spun back around. "Why does it matter if anybody—"

"Go. Now," she ordered, crossing her arms in front of her chest. "And don't come back until you have an answer."

Then she pulled the door firmly closed, the lock clicking into place with an emphatic *thud*.

6

———

The hot Carolina sun was already beating against the concrete as I lugged the box out to the car. It shone through the trees in sneaky spears, and I hissed when I emerged from the shadow of an oak tree into a bright patch next to the street.

When I reached up to shield my eyes from the glare, something small and feathery darted across the street toward me. It made a loud squawk, and in a momentary bout of terror, I stumbled backward over the edge of the curb and screamed.

The box of Rocky's things tumbled to the asphalt in slow motion, and I watched in horror as his youth baseball trophy snapped in half upon impact. Photos rained to the ground, and stacks of paper fluttered onto the dried-up grass.

I glanced back at the house just in time to see my grandmother shake her head and press the newspaper curtains back into place.

When something nipped at my toe, I glanced down to find the offending streak of fluff: a black and white speckled chicken that reminded me of a walking Oreo. I brushed him aside with the tip of my flip-flop, and he responded by letting loose a flurry of sharp clucks that reminded me of Beverlee when I stole the last snickerdoodle from her chicken-shaped cookie jar.

After he finished his tiny tantrum, my new friend got distracted by a matchbook from a local dive bar. I used a tattered second place ribbon that had landed near the sewer drain to keep him from lighting himself on fire.

"Who are you?"

I looked up to find a small child leaning against the front fender of the car. He had dirty bare feet and a purple Popsicle ring around his lips. The offending treat dripped down his chin and onto his t-shirt.

"And why are you messing with Phil?" he went on before I could answer.

"The chicken's name is Phil?"

He nodded eagerly. "Yes. My grandma loved some guy on television named Phil Donahue."

I compared the affable, white-haired talk show host from the eighties to the feisty bird that was pecking at my pinky while making *buck-buck-buck* noises. "Sorry. I don't see it."

"I'm Brian," he said, biting the last piece of his Popsicle and slurping the juice off his fingers.

"Glory," I responded. "Glory Wells."

Brian pointed toward Ada's house. "Do you live here now?"

"No, I'm just visiting. Ada is my grandmother."

"Does she like Phil Donahue, too?" he asked with a tilted head, his floppy sun-streaked hair falling over his eyes.

I wrinkled up my nose. "I don't really know."

"Do you live near here?" he asked, continuing his

running chatter. "I don't. I live in Charlotte, but I'm here visiting Grandpa for the day. My mom said he gets lonely sometimes since he retired from driving, so I'm supposed to cheer him—"

"Brian!" A voice boomed from behind an azalea next door. "I told you not to leave the yard."

Brian grinned and pointed toward the side yard with his Popsicle stick. "That's Grandpa Bud."

A pink-cheeked older gentleman appeared at the edge of the weeds wearing oil-stained overalls and wiping his brow with a shop towel. "You were supposed to stay with the lawnmower while I ran inside for a screwdriver."

The little boy shrugged. "Phil made a run for it, and I tried to save him from getting squashed by a car."

"That rooster is just searching for a lady friend again. He's much less likely to get run over than you are." Grandpa Bud swatted Brian with the towel and gave him a patient smile. "So next time, stay put."

Bud turned to me and reached out a hand. "I see you've met our neighborhood chicken Lothario and my very sticky grandson. I'm Bud Perkins."

Returning his smile, I took his palm in mine. It was warm and scratchy, and for a moment, I let myself get lost in the idea of having a grandfather of my own. "I'm Glory. Glory Wells."

"She's Ada's granddaughter," Brian supplied. "But she doesn't know if Ada likes Phil Donahue or not."

"You're the Boyd girl," Bud said softly. A shadow crossed his face, and a deep line furrowed his brow.

The Boyd girl.

I was familiar with the nickname. As a child, the people of Flat Falls used it as a descriptor, the same way they would have if I was the spawn of a drug lord or a vegan.

Which was why Beverlee had changed my last name to

Wells as quickly as she could get the adoption papers signed. She had wanted me to carry on my mother's last name instead of constantly having to overcome my father's.

"It's Wells, actually," I replied. "I don't go by Boyd."

Bud's lips had formed into a thin line. "It's time to go, Brian. Let's grab Phil and get back to the house."

"We can't," Brian said, pointing to the mess on the ground. "We have to help Glory clean up because she wouldn't have dropped it if Phil hadn't scared her to begin with. And you said we should always help a lady in distress, because you never know—"

Bud clamped a hand over Brian's mouth.

"That's okay," I said, offering an out from the wave of discomfort that had pushed its way into our conversation. "I've got it."

"No, he's right. Forgive my lack of manners." Bud leaned over and plucked a photo off the ground. He inspected it for a moment before holding it out to me. He gestured toward the picture. "Sorry to hear about your uncle. I'll bet it came as quite a surprise."

"That's an understatement," I muttered, taking the photo between my fingers. It was an old snapshot of Burton and Virginia Levi, although from the graduation attire they were wearing, it was taken before they got married. They both wore royal blue robes and flat-topped caps, and in one hand, Burton held a bubbling bottle of cheap champagne. His other arm was wrapped firmly around his future wife's shoulders.

Off to one side of the picture, my uncle stood with his arms fisted in his own robe, his eyes focused on Virginia.

Virginia Levi was a hot commodity.

Bud finished scooping up the photos and handed them to me, and then reached down for a pile of old sketchbooks. He flipped open one of the covers, then slammed it shut, a blush creeping up his cheeks. He thrust it toward me and cleared his throat.

Curious, I opened to a random page, which was filled with sketches of naked women.

My uncle liked to draw boobs. Awesome. Good to know I came from such classy stock.

I held the sketchbook in the air. "We can't all be Picasso," I said, my voice a little too bright. I dropped it in the box, pulled the lid closed, and plopped it onto the passenger seat.

When I turned to say goodbye, Bud and Brian were gone.

7

———

I returned to the office by way of the gas station, which took longer than I expected since I had to stop for a doughnut, and I couldn't figure out how to open the gas tank in Scoots's fancy muscle car.

I sighed as I thought about my Honda. I never had to fight her gas tank to open. Or her doors. In fact, the passenger door flew open on its own once when I was driving around downtown Raleigh. It took out a parking meter and left a good-sized scrape on the sign for my favorite Thai restaurant.

Unfortunately, driving and eating were a dangerous combination, and when I sat at a red light on the edge of town, half the strawberry jelly squirted out the back of the doughnut onto my white blouse, leaving a bright red stain. I didn't have time to go home and change, so I headed into the office to find a stain stick and discovered Virginia and Totty, the mom brigade, waiting for me in the lobby.

Totty wore a tailored peach pantsuit, her chin-length blond bob tucked behind her ears to display the pair of M&M-sized pearl earrings Moe bought her after he won his third term as mayor. But that was where her put-together appearance ended. Her stockings featured a prominent run at the ankle, and she hadn't even bothered to buckle the strap of one of her sandals. It flapped against her foot as her crossed leg bobbed along to the music from the speaker on Beverlee's desk.

As the clock ticked down toward her daughter's wedding, the more frazzled she became, often showing up for planning sessions in my office with her three-inch binder and stack of color-coded index cards in total disarray. Even with all the pre-printed labels and Pinterest-worthy organizational hacks, she never managed to find anything when she needed it.

It was nothing new, though. Totty had been showing up in disheveled outfits and mismatched shoes since I was a child. She'd even arrived at my fifth-grade graduation in a lovely floral blouse and a silk slip because she had gotten distracted by a phone call while getting dressed and forgot to put on a skirt. Moe called her forgetfulness *charming*, but he still had his secretary check that his wife was fully clothed before every event.

Virginia Levi, on the other hand, was the picture of understated elegance. Her gray leather tote matched a linen shift dress that fell to just below her knees. Shiny brown hair that didn't dare sprout a thread of silver was held back in a sleek low ponytail, and she referred to the iPad in her lap so often I began to wonder if she was running the space program from it.

I forced a smile, reeling the box in tight to cover my shirt. "Good afternoon, ladies. Did we have a meeting scheduled?"

Virginia tucked her tablet in her bag and rose to greet me. "You've got your hands full. Are those the menu plaques for the luncheon?"

Burton had insisted that the residents of Flat Falls weren't intelligent enough to differentiate between the items on the buffet table, so we had ordered custom cards so the guests wouldn't get confused. "No, they came in yesterday. This is just some stuff I grabbed from my grandmother's house."

"Can I help you with the box?" Virginia asked.

"I would say yes," I replied, juggling the box to cover the stain on my shirt, "but I'm hiding a spot on my blouse. I was hoping to sneak into the back to change before you noticed."

Totty rushed forward and peered over the lid. "That's nothing. I once let a stylist talk me into wearing a white sundress to a rally in the middle of August." She fanned herself. "You ladies know how hot it gets around here in the summer. By the time Moe got up to speak, I had sweated through every inch of that dress, and we had to fashion a shawl from a checkered tablecloth we stole from the water table to keep from giving the donors in the front row an eyeful they didn't pay for."

I acquiesced, dropping the box on Beverlee's desk. "Make yourselves comfortable in the conference room, and I'll be right with you."

I motioned for Beverlee to meet me in the back and nudged the door closed with my hip. I pulled the shirt away from my chest, cringing when the dried jelly pulled at my skin like an old bandage. "I can't go back out there like this. I look like I've been shot."

"Might get you out of a meeting if you need to go to the emergency room," she suggested.

I pinned her with a glare.

"Fine." She unbuttoned her orange cardigan and held it out to me. "Put this on."

Aside from being the color of a traffic cone, it also had

several layers of ruffles in places where sweaters shouldn't have ruffles. But I didn't have another choice, so I slipped it on and buttoned it up. "I look like one of those push-up sherbet pops you used to buy me from the ice cream truck."

Beverly snorted. "You would only look like sherbet if you showed a little bit more cleavage." I wiggled my shoulders, wishing I had magic powers to make sweaters increase in size. Beverlee was every bit as tall as me, and a size or two larger.

Unfortunately, her clothing wasn't.

"These are clients, not dates," I replied.

"Don't be so quick to shut down the possibilities," Beverly said. "Totty's got a nephew who sells shoes at the department store over in Siler City."

"He also has an arrest record for stealing pork rinds from the gas station," I whispered, looking over at the door to make sure Totty couldn't hear us. "I think I'll pass."

Beverlee shrugged. "A good shoe discount can go a long way toward making me forgive a man for his transgressions."

Beverlee was always encouraging me to find a husband. Or a one-night stand. It didn't matter, as long as I wasn't sitting home alone with my face buried in a carton of ice cream while watching true crime documentaries. But since she had already been through a few husbands herself, I didn't think she was the one I should turn to for marital advice.

Besides, I had already been married, and it didn't turn out well the first time. I wasn't convinced it would work the second time, either.

I adjusted the sweater to hide the stain the best I could, then tucked my hair behind my ears and marched back out to the conference room, where Totty and Virginia were flipping through a stack of bridal magazines.

"Sorry for the delay. I had to run an errand in Big River this morning, so I wasn't expecting visitors." I pasted on my best keep-the-clients-happy smile. "But I'm always delighted to see the two of you. What can I help you with today?"

"Totty and I were just chatting about the reception," Virginia said as she whipped out her tablet and swiped through several screens. She no doubt had word-for-word transcripts of every conversation we'd had since Ruby accepted that two carat pink diamond from her son eight months prior. "And we wanted to make sure that you weren't sitting the preacher from Flat Falls Baptist Church next to Father Ryan from Big River."

Totty nodded in emphatic agreement. "You would think those two could be friendly, but there was a disagreement at Old Man Pritchard's funeral, and something ended up on fire."

Old Man Pritchard was a peeping Tom who died from falling out a second-story window after trying to catch the high school volleyball coach in the shower. If I had to guess, I would imagine it was his soul that went ablaze.

I opened the file that contained the seating chart and turned my laptop around, pointing out that the preacher and the priest were seated on opposite sides of the room, with more than enough old ladies in between to occupy them with stories of their aches and pains for most of the afternoon.

"Good, good." Totty grinned at Virginia. "See, I told you she had it under control."

"We were just worried when we weren't able to get in touch with you this morning," Virginia said. "We heard you might be over in Big River, and we wanted to make sure everything was okay with the wedding plans, given your recent family issues."

"I was paying a visit to my grandmother," I replied. "The discovery of Rocky's death came as a shock to us all." That, and the ridiculous notion that my father was somehow involved, had kept me up late for the last few nights.

"We are all so sorry to hear of your uncle's passing." Totty rested her hand on my forearm. "And I've got a casserole in my refrigerator for you. With extra cheese because I know it's your favorite."

There were very few times in my life I had refused anything with extra cheese, but Totty's cooking was the stuff of legends. Many Flat Falls residents had regretted the gastrointestinal distress one of her sympathy dishes had brought.

I summoned a grateful smile, even though I'd deposit her gift straight into the dumpster. Not even Rusty, our neighborhood golden retriever, would touch it.

❧

SEVERAL DAYS of running around Flat Falls preparing last-minute wedding details had worn me out, so I took the next morning to sleep in.

That meant putting on my coziest sweatpants, throwing my hair in a messy bun, and setting the coffee maker to brew an enormous pot of caffeine to be ready when I rolled out of bed, bleary-eyed, at the crack of noon.

Unfortunately, a loud banging at the front door woke me up before eight. When crushing a pillow to my head didn't make it stop, I stumbled to the door and threw it open without even checking the peephole. I expected to find Beverlee on the other side with a muffin from the Grind and Go and a plan to coerce me into helping her create a man-attracting garden behind her shed. Her craziest plans always arrived first thing in the morning.

Instead, a short, balding man in a police uniform stood there, his hat pressed across his abundant belly. I didn't recognize him from my many visits to the Flat Falls police station, and his uniform was navy instead of khaki. He wore a shiny metal name badge across his chest that read W. Daly.

"Can I help you?" I asked, reaching across to the entry table where I had dropped my cardigan on the way into the apartment the night before. I shrugged into it, folding my arms and waiting for my visitor to introduce himself and provide some sort of valid reason for waking me up from a delicious dream about a sexy Italian stranger and an all-you-can-eat ice cream buffet.

"Sorry to bother you this early in the morning, ma'am. But I have some important business, and I needed to get started on it before the festival crowds get too busy."

"And you are?"

He looked at his feet and then back up at me with an awkward smile that made his mustache wobble. "Sorry. The name is Wayne Daly."

"What can I do for you this morning, Mr. Daly? It's a little early for a social call."

"It's Chief," he replied, fumbling in his pocket for his shield. "Chief Daly. And I'm here to ask you a few questions about the body you uncovered a few days ago. Do you mind if I come in?"

I studied him for a second, then realized he was about six inches shorter than me, and I could probably take him in a fight, so I nudged the door open with my elbow. "I've got a lot going on with the wedding today, and I don't have much time."

It was a lie, but if I was going to get murdered by a

stranger in my living room, I wanted him to think he had a deadline.

He nodded, and his eyes swept the room. "It won't take long. I was reviewing the details of the recent accident in town, and I was wondering if you could tell me more about what you saw when you dislodged the statue and uncovered the remains."

We could have been talking about how sweet the tomatoes were down at the Food Barn judging by his nonchalant tone, as if ramming your car into a statue and finding a leather-wearing corpse happened every day.

"I already told Hollis everything."

He nodded slowly. "I understand, but Chief Goodnight and I don't always see eye to eye on investigations. I thought it might be better for me to come down here and talk to you myself. In case he missed something."

I flashed back to the image of my bumper resting next to what appeared to be a foot, and my stomach swirled. "There were… remains. In leather."

Chief Daly gave an acknowledging grunt. "I understand you knew the deceased."

"He was my uncle, if that's what you mean. But I didn't really know him. He has been gone since I was a kid, and I don't even remember him before that."

Chief Daly made a slow circle around the room, his gaze scraping every surface. I was just about to ask him what he found so fascinating about the pile of wedding magazines and the abandoned pretzel bag on my coffee table when Beverlee burst through the open door with so much force that it slammed into the wall behind her.

"Wayne Daly," she said, her fist propped on her hip. "What, pray tell, are you doing in my niece's apartment?"

Chief Daly cleared his throat and adjusted the collar of

his shirt. "Beverlee," he said, reaching out to grab her hand, then slowly raising it to his lips. "It's great to see you."

She tugged her hand away and wiped the back of it on her sunny yellow tracksuit. "Of course it is. Now answer the question."

Chief Daly stepped backward. "Your niece? I can definitely see the resemblance. You're both lovely, and you haven't aged a bit since last we met."

His brows wiggled as he made the last statement, and I wasn't sure if it was because he was flirting or if he had some sort of tic. Either way, Beverlee wasn't having any of it.

"Don't start with me, Wayne," she said, a frown crossing her lips. "I was waiting in line for my cappuccino at the Grind and Go when word got out you had slithered into town. Naturally, I had to scurry over here to make sure you didn't have any ill intentions toward my dear Glory."

I snorted. "Beverlee, I don't think—"

She pinned me with a glare before twisting around to face him. "We have our own police chief in Flat Falls, and he's perfectly capable of handling the investigation without you sticking your nose in where it doesn't belong."

"You always did have a thing for him," Wayne replied, his expression darkening. "But just because your niece found the body in Flat Falls doesn't mean Hollis Goodnight has jurisdiction."

"That's exactly what it means." Hollis stood at the door. The mid-morning sun shone behind him, and he was silhouetted in the doorframe. With his wide-legged stance and his arms casually positioned at his hips, he could have been a Wild West gunslinger, and I glanced over his shoulder, half-expecting to see a shady guy with a harmonica following him up the stairs.

"Hollis," Wayne said in greeting, tipping his head toward the other man.

"Wayne." Hollis stepped forward, giving both Beverlee and me a cursory inspection to ensure that we were unharmed. "What brings you to Flat Falls this early in the morning?"

"I heard you found the body of one of my citizens," Wayne replied, his uneasy gaze bouncing between Beverlee and the exterior stairs.

"We found a body, yes." Before Wayne could respond, Hollis held up a finger to silence him. "But we haven't confirmed his identity yet."

Hollis positioned himself between us and Wayne, then slowly moved toward the door, essentially pushing the other man toward the exit. "If we do confirm that he's one of yours, I'll be sure to have my detectives reach out to your department as a courtesy."

The Flat Falls police chief had been a fixture around my life since I was a child, but I had never seen him look so stern. Even the time I ran away, and he found me hanging out at the biker bar on the edge of town with a twenty-three-year-old who had a rap sheet longer than my forearm, he still managed to crack a smile.

Now, though, his face was drawn, and a furrow creased the area between his brows. Once he had shepherded Chief Daly out onto the porch, he turned back and gave Beverlee a single nod, then closed the door behind him.

Beverlee released an annoyed sigh and slumped down on the sofa. "You don't happen to have a cappuccino, do you? I need to wash the taste of testosterone out of my mouth."

I crossed to the kitchen and canceled the timer on the coffee pot so it would start immediately. When it gave a displeased hiss and the pot started to brew, I called out to Beverlee. "What was that all about?"

"There's a history between those two," she responded. "And not a good one."

I plucked two mugs from the cabinet and set them out on the counter before returning to the living room. "It seemed serious. What are they fighting over?"

"Me," she replied nonchalantly, her sandal dangling off her tangerine-painted big toe.

I dropped onto the seat next to her. "Please tell me you didn't date Deputy Dork."

She lifted a shoulder. "I wouldn't exactly call it dating. But he did have really strong arm muscles for such a little man. Came in handy when we—"

I raised my hand to silence her. "Stop. Right now."

She chuckled. "It was a long time ago."

"I would hope so. But I'm curious about something. How did Hollis know he was here?"

"I called him, of course. While I was on my way over here from the coffee shop."

"Why?" I asked. "He seemed innocent enough."

"Wayne Daly is anything but innocent," she said. "And I figured he'd be sniffing around town after you uncovered Rocky's body."

"Did he and Rocky know each other?"

The coffeemaker beeped, and she jumped up. "Know each other? Yes. Like each other? Absolutely not. Those two were mortal enemies. My guess is he came to town for proof that Rocky was actually buried beneath that statue."

"Why would he need proof?"

"So he could finally breathe," she replied. "He's been waiting for Rocky to show up and shoot him dead for years."

8

Later that morning, I received a call that Burton Levi was downtown making the mayor's personal assistant cry.

She had been carefully following our site plan for the luncheon, directing the delivery of the tables and chairs, when Burton burst onto the scene declaring that round tables were tacky and claiming that only an idiot would think of using them during lunch.

After calling me in tears, she waited on the sidewalk with her clipboard. When I crossed the street, she rushed forward as if I had just brought her a winning lottery ticket or a bucket full of calorie-free chocolate.

"Thank goodness you're here," she said through a fresh wave of sniffles. "That man is scary."

I could hear Burton's booming voice easily over the sounds of squealing children and carnival music revving up for the day. I squared my shoulders and pushed my way into the tent. He was easy to locate, standing in the center of the space yelling while everyone else cowered along the canvas walls and avoided eye contact.

"Good morning, Mr. Levi," I called out with forced enthusiasm. "I understand you have some concerns about the tables we have chosen for the luncheon." I motioned for him to follow me to an uncrowded part of the tent. "Let's have a seat so we can talk through your concerns."

Burton followed me across the tent with his wife trailing behind him. When I motioned for him to sit, he narrowed his eyes and crossed his arms, but remained standing.

"Okay, then," I said, mustering up a smile, "why don't you start by telling me what's on your mind?"

"What's on my mind is that you and your team are a bunch of dimwits."

The color drained from Virginia's cheeks, but she didn't say anything.

Beverlee always said that you catch more flies being sweet than you do punching someone in the gut, so I dug my fingernail into my palm to keep from releasing a string of unmannerly curses.

I took a fortifying breath. "I take it you prefer square tables?"

"Anybody with half a brain knows that square tables are better for this type of event."

I cracked my knuckles, then stuffed my hands in my pocket before it became apparent I was fantasizing about tossing one of those offensive round tables over onto his shiny black loafer. "Mr. Levi, we had to consider a number of factors when making the decision. The bride wanted the room to have a more intimate feel that allows for a more organic flow of guests. We can also fit more tables into the area if they are round—"

"You don't know what you're talking about." He motioned to his wife's ever-present tablet, which rested on the table in front of her. "What's the name of that other wedding planner? The one named after a tree."

There were only two wedding planners in Flat Falls. Most of the time I referred to the other one as She-Devil, but that was only when I was feeling generous. "I believe you're thinking about Magnolia Winters."

"She has more experience with events like this than you do. She's held quite a few of them in my restaurant, in fact," Burton sneered.

I didn't doubt that. Maggie was a well-respected wedding planner whose client list was easily ten times longer than mine.

She was also wretched and had been tormenting me since elementary school.

And I wasn't the only one. Ruby Fowler had been her target in high school as well, and the only reason she agreed to get married during the festival was that the mayor promised Maggie would play no part in planning the wedding. The last I'd heard, he had put her in charge of the clowns that would be running around the funhouse, which I thought was an excellent use of her talents.

"Thank you for your suggestion, Mr. Levi," I said, pulling out my *you're-a-moron-but-you're-paying-the-bills* voice. "But I assure you Magnolia would tell you the same thing. Round tables are simply the more prudent choice for this event."

And I would also rather pry my own tongue out with a cheese spreader than work with her on another wedding.

Fortunately, Burton didn't put up an argument, because one of his employees chose that moment to come bustling into the tent. His crisp white apron had wide red streaks, like a can of tomatoes had just exploded in his face, and his cheeks were flushed beneath a close-cropped auburn beard that matched his man bun. He was out of breath and seemed to be about thirty seconds from a panic attack.

He leaned in close and spoke to Burton in frantic whispers while gesturing toward the makeshift kitchen.

When Burton didn't respond immediately, I looked at his wife. Her fingers were white from clutching the tablet, and her eyes were wide.

Finally, Burton broke the tense silence. "Very well," he said, his voice low and calm. "Then you're fired, Oliver."

Oliver pressed his hand to the front of his starched white apron. "Again?"

Burton lunged forward, his gaze full of fire. He pointed toward the exit. "Get out. Now. And don't let me ever see you in my restaurant again."

Oliver hesitated for a moment before storming away with clenched fists.

Virginia stood and rushed over to her husband. "You can't do that, Burton. Oliver French has worked for you for fifteen years. And before that, he worked for your father. He's as much a part of Lavish as you are."

"Do not tell me how to run my restaurant. I don't tolerate insolence," he said with a scowl, striding out through the tent's flap without even glancing over his shoulder.

Virginia offered me a quick apology. "I'm so sorry. He's under a lot of pressure to make the day perfect for Ruby and Warren. You wouldn't believe the number of details he has to keep straight."

I returned her tight-lipped smile and bit back a retort. "Of course. Tensions always rise right before the big day."

That was true, but the drama usually involved something like the bride bickering with a groomsman over whether it was appropriate to bring an exotic dancer he'd met at the bachelor party as his plus one, not whether I should consider issuing a restraining order on the groom's father.

After I convinced Virginia to let the round tables remain in the luncheon tent because we couldn't get replacements before the next day, I spent hours sifting through old photographs and searching through the Flat Falls newspaper archives online. I was no closer to figuring out who had killed Rocky Boyd. So I asked for help.

My reinforcements arrived with large cups of coffee and two bags of crullers from the gas station.

Beverlee strolled into the apartment in a fifties-style sailor dress with a flouncy navy skirt and a wide red patent leather belt cinched tight at her waist. A matching scarf was knotted through her hair, and before she even greeted me, she paused in front of the mirror to touch up her lip gloss.

Scoots muscled past her, an oversized flannel shirt flapping open over faded denim overalls with grass stains on the knees. Purple high-top tennis shoes that matched the tips of her short, spiky hair finished off her eclectic ensemble.

I tried to hide a grin as she tapped two packets of sugar into her coffee.

"What are you looking at?" she demanded, tossing an

annoyed glare over her shoulder before rifling through the donuts.

"Nothing," I replied. "You just look cute."

She slammed her coffee cup onto the table, not even wincing when a healthy splash bounced out onto the overalls. "Cute?" she asked, giving me a look of disgust, as if I had just mopped her floor with a kitten. "There's nothing cute about me."

I shook my head. "No, of course not. You look mean. Dangerous, even. People will think you're our bodyguard. Or, you know, a farmer on her way to plant some bulbs or milk a wayward cow."

Just then, the door opened, and Josie ambled in, saving me from whatever violence lived on the other side of Scoot's scowl. She dropped onto the sofa and grabbed my laptop, kicking out her leg to expose the plastic monitor still wrapped around her ankle.

Josie had been on house arrest for a white-collar crime she didn't intentionally commit—yet another nod to the not-so-noble husbands of the world—and we were counting down the days until she could join us out in the world again.

"You can't have much longer," Beverlee said. "You've been in that thing for ages. Surely you get time off for good behavior."

Aside from being beautiful, with long strawberry blond hair and a figure that belied the quantity of pizza she regularly ate, our friendly neighborhood criminal still enjoyed sticking her digital nose in other people's business. But now she had to sneak around to do it, so any time she was going to snoop, Josie used my login. Somewhere off in cyberland, there was probably a record of me doing a lot of things that were borderline illegal.

Josie tapped her ankle. "Two months. Then you have to

promise to let me tag along on your adventures. Until then, what do you want me to do while you guys are gallivanting around looking for bad guys?"

"Stay here and look for bad guys," I replied. "See if you can find any reason Burton would kill his best friend."

She hopped up, taking the laptop with her. "On it."

We followed her out the door. Just before we descended to the alley below, Scoots held out her hand, palm up.

"Gimme," she said.

I feigned innocence. I knew she wanted the keys to the Mustang, but Scoots drove like someone had lit her tailpipe on fire. I didn't relish spending the rest of the morning in jail because she had mouthed off to a police officer while driving seventy miles an hour and weaving between vacationers on the causeway.

I sent a pleading gaze to Beverlee, who was staring, wide-eyed at the sports car.

"Nope." Beverlee descended the rickety metal stairs. "The last time I let you drive me anywhere, we had to get pulled out of a ditch. I was queasy for days."

Scoots elbowed past her. "That wasn't my fault. That squirrel came out of nowhere. And besides, I thought you enjoyed your personal visit with the handsome young paramedics who so valiantly came to our rescue."

"They were very strapping," she admitted.

While Beverlee reminisced, I dropped onto the driver's seat and held up the keys in triumph. "Sorry to break it to you, but we're not going ditch diving today, ladies. Hop in."

Beverlee stuck out her bottom lip in a fake pout as she climbed into the back seat. "But... paramedics, Glory. You know how I love a man in uniform."

"And you're willing to damage the car and risk your life just to see one?" I asked, studying her in the rearview mirror.

"Maybe."

Scoots slid into the passenger seat and closed the door with a little more force than necessary. "I'm only letting you drive so I can watch for clues. There's no telling what we'll find once we cross the border."

~

BEVERLEE BELIEVED that crossing the bridge into Big River was much like passing into the netherworld, and I could see her wary scowl as the car bounced over the speed bump at the edge of town. She practically dislocated her shoulder waving at everyone she passed in Flat Falls, but she didn't even lift a finger when a woman in a bright pink tennis skirt waved at us from the sidewalk.

"Huh," I said, flashing a knowing glance toward Beverlee in the mirror. "The lady walking her Pomeranian just waved to me like a normal neighbor. I thought everybody in this town was a heathen bent on destroying other people's souls."

Beverlee shrugged. "She must be new."

I had just begun to think this feud was a ridiculous mistake when I heard the siren's first wail. I glanced into the mirror to see a black SUV with flashing lights quickly approaching from behind.

I flipped the blinker and pulled to the shoulder to let him pass.

Unfortunately, he followed me.

"Why are you stopping?" Scoots asked.

"I'm getting pulled over. That's what you do."

Scoots rolled her eyes and folded her arms across her chest. "I'm disappointed in you. You had plenty of time to floor it. By the time he realized you were gone, you could have been halfway back home."

"I'm not running from a police officer," I replied through gritted teeth.

The rebellious part of me wanted to agree with her, to throw the Mustang into gear and see how loud the squeals were as I tested the limits of this sports car. But the practical part of me—the one who made sure I paid my taxes on time and never washed my lights and darks in the same load—kept her foot firmly planted on the brake pedal.

Once upon a time, I would have given that officer a run for his money. But not today. Today, I crossed my hands in my lap and watched him hike up his pants before he began his slow, deliberate march up to the driver's side door. When he got closer, I recognized him.

I rolled the window down and lifted my hand in greeting. "Chief Daly, it's lovely to see you again so soon."

He slid mirrored sunglasses to the tip of his nose and peered down at me. "I wish I could say the same thing about you, Miss Wells, but it appears you and your fancy car lack respect for the laws of our little town. We've had a bit of a crime wave lately. Somebody tried to break into the library just yesterday, and I've given my staff the instruction to look for any interlopers who come to Big River looking to break the rules."

Scoots stiffened in the passenger seat, and I reached over to give her forearm a reassuring squeeze. "I'm not sure what you're talking about. We just arrived in town, and we haven't broken any—"

He punched his pointer finger into the air. "One," he said. "I received a call from Debbie Grace Dixon advising me that a car matching this description was far exceeding the speed limit over on Pullenville Road."

He leaned in close enough for me to see the individual hairs trying to escape from his nostrils. "That's a school zone, Miss Wells. In case you were too busy racing through my town to notice all the yellow signs."

"We didn't—"

"And two," he interrupted, flipping up a second finger. "I have another witness who saw you blow through a stop sign in front of the Piggly Wiggly. I'm not sure if you noticed the billboard, but Tuesday is senior citizens' day at our little grocery store, and to hear that you willingly endangered some of our beloved elderly residents who only wanted to grab a warm lunch makes my blood practically volcanic."

I hadn't been anywhere near the Piggly Wiggly, much less chased down an old lady with a chicken pot pie. I was about to confront the chief on his misinformation when a loud sigh and a frantic banging came from the back seat.

"Glory," Beverlee said, smacking her palm against the glass window. "If you would be so kind as to release the child locks and take your leave, I need to have a brief word with Wayne."

She patiently waited while I stumbled out of the driver's seat, but as soon as I hit the pavement and nudged the lever to free her from the back, she bolted out onto the sidewalk.

I shot Scoots an alarmed look, but she just dipped her chin and allowed a slight smile to lift the corners of her mouth as she craned her neck to look past me out the window.

"Wayne Daly," Beverlee said in her sweetest voice.

I swallowed. When Beverlee turned up the heat on her drawl, I knew somebody was about to get a bless-your-heart beat down. "I can't imagine where you get your information, but it's incorrect. You know my niece didn't do any of those things you accused her of."

He cleared his throat. "It's Chief. Chief Daly."

Beverlee dismissed his announcement with a quick flick

of her wrist, resting her palm on his starched uniform sleeve.

His eyes went wide, and he reached for the radio strapped to his waistband. But before he could make the call that he had been accosted by a crazy lady with big hair and frosty pink lip gloss, she stepped in even closer.

"Listen here, Wayne," she said, moving her finger to the center of his chest. "You might have thought you were a big shot back in high school when you used to cram all the band kids in their lockers, but we're not in high school anymore, and you don't get to bully people just for the fun of it."

She kept her finger in place and turned to face me. "He once stuck your daddy and his trumpet in a gym locker and left him there all day. I don't even want to think about how smelly that was. It must have been like living inside a dumpster. And Wayne didn't even get reprimanded." Then her voice changed into a singsong tone, and she bobbed her head back and forth. "Because his father was the police chief."

Chief Daly stumbled backward, struggling to regain his composure. "I'm the chief now, Beverlee. And this is my town."

"Well, then," Beverlee replied with a satisfied nod. "You should do a better job of welcoming your neighbors."

With that, she slid back into the car and tapped my headrest twice. I caught her gaze through the rear window.

Go, she mouthed.

My jaw dropped, but I hopped into the driver's seat, put the car in drive, and gave Chief Daly a jaunty wave. "Have a nice day."

When I veered around the corner to head into downtown Big River, he was still standing on the side of the road, his hands fisted at his sides.

10

Scoots let out a whoop and patted the shiny dashboard of the Mustang as I pulled to a stop in front of my grandmother's house. "Thatta girl. I always knew you had it in you."

"Are you talking to me?" I asked.

She snorted. "As if. You drive like an old lady. I'm talking about the car. George always babied her, like he was afraid to let her be free and let her hair loose. He'd lose his spleen if he saw her now. A respectable roadster doesn't run from the cops."

"Neither does a respectable citizen." I cast a worried look over my shoulder, half-expecting a fleet of cops to come barreling down the road any second. "I'm going to be arrested."

Beverlee's snicker echoed through the car. "You're not going to be arrested. Wayne Daly has too many skeletons in his closet, and I'm sure I know more than half of them. He's not going to mess with you."

"And you didn't even run," Scoots added. "You

sashayed. You might as well have tooted your horn and thrown rose petals out the window. Once upon a time, you would have left rubber on the road, and he'd be smelling like your exhaust for a week."

Beverlee agreed with an exuberant nod. "It's hard to believe you're the same girl who I had to pick up from the police station after you were caught drag racing at three o'clock in the morning wearing a polka-dotted bikini top and a pair of cut-off jean shorts."

I remembered that outfit. I'd give just about anything to pull it off these days, but I had developed too much of a fondness for tacos. "That was a long time ago."

"Not that long," she said quietly, giving my shoulder a gentle squeeze. "She's still in there."

Before I let Beverlee venture too deep into psychoanalyzing my journey from teenage rebel to pearls-wearing business owner, I pointed toward the front of Ada's house. "Why don't we focus our energy on figuring out what happened between Rocky and my dad on the night my parents died?"

Scoots nodded. "So you think she knows something?"

"I'm sure of it," I replied. "But what I don't know is why she wouldn't just tell me while I was there. What's the big secret?"

I caught a glance between Scoots and Beverlee in my rearview mirror.

"Enough with the looks. What aren't you telling me?"

Scoots opened the car door and jumped out, lifting her brows toward Beverlee in her this-is-on-you-face. "I'll just be out here," she said, motioning around the yard. "Hanging out with the dead grass."

She slammed the door, and the sound resonated through the silence.

I looked into the mirror, but Beverlee was avoiding eye contact, her fingers tapping on the armrest as she chewed her bottom lip.

I knew from experience that she was going to blow in three… two… one…

She let out a dramatic sigh and fluttered her hand to her chest. "I just can't."

Alarm prickled at the back of my neck. If this was any ordinary secret, she would have put up her false front of honor, then practically climbed over the seat in her enthusiasm to spill it. But this time, her lips pressed together in a tight line, and a glaze of tears reddened her eyes.

I opened the car door and stepped out, gesturing for her to do the same. When we were both standing on the sidewalk, I dipped my head low to meet her gaze. "Talk," I instructed.

She brushed her sandal against a clump of dirt, watching it scatter before finally speaking. "I ran into Hollis earlier today."

"Did he have news about Rocky?"

"He was asking about your mother's jewelry."

I wrinkled my brow. "I don't understand."

"Lucy was one of those natural beauties who didn't need fancy clothes or makeup." When Beverlee looked back up, those unshed tears from a few moments earlier had begun to make their way down her cheeks. "And she didn't wear a lot of jewelry, either."

"Okay," I said slowly. "What does that have to do with Hollis?"

"She only wore jewelry when it was sentimental to her. Things like her wedding ring and…"

My blood pressure rose with every second that passed. "And? Go on."

Beverlee released a whoosh of breath. "And a locket with a family picture in it."

A faint memory floated through the back of my mind as I pictured my mother's smiling face in the photos that lined Beverlee's bookshelves. In most of them, a silver locket was wound around her neck.

"She never went anywhere without it," Beverlee said. "She always told me it was her way of carrying you with her when you were apart. You and your daddy gave it to her for Mother's Day during your first year of school. She picked it out from the fundraising catalog and then showed it off to everyone in town like she was wearing the crown jewels."

"I remember," I replied, a lump forming in my throat.

"Hollis said they found something closed up tight in Rocky's fist."

I gasped. "Mama's—"

Beverlee nodded, wiping another tear as it trailed down her cheek, leaving a stream of black mascara in its wake. "It appears Rocky was holding Lucy's locket when he died."

"But why?" Confusion swirling through my head, I reached out to steady myself on the hood of the car. "I don't understand. Why did Rocky have it?"

Beverlee's fist closed around the collar of her shirt. She pulled it away from her skin, as if she was willing more air to fill her chest. "Baby, you knew your daddy and Rocky were fighting the night your parents died, right?"

I didn't trust myself to speak, so I simply nodded.

"Hollis has a witness who says they were fighting over someone."

"A woman?" I asked, still unable to comprehend what she was dancing around. "What woman?"

She brushed her knuckles against my cheek in a whisper-gentle touch. "Glory, your daddy thought you hung the moon."

"I know. And he loved Mama that much, too. So I don't understand why they were fighting over her."

"They weren't fighting over her," she replied. "They were fighting over you. Hollis believes that Rocky and Daniel were fighting because they had just found out that Rocky was your father." The next few minutes passed in a blur. Beverlee grabbed me under the armpits and practically dragged me to my grandmother's front porch, then fanned me with a wide palm frond she ripped clean off the tree next to the driveway.

"I practically burned Hollis's ear off with the talking-to I gave him." She continued babbling, nervous energy making her words come out in frantic bursts. "I told him there was no way Lucy would have cheated on your daddy. Absolutely no way."

Ada's front yard closed in on me, then expanded back out again. I stumbled toward Ada's steps, and vaguely heard knocking as Beverlee pounded on the front door. "Open up, old woman. Your granddaughter needs you."

When my grandmother didn't even crack the door, Beverlee trotted down the porch and started calling for Scoots, who had disappeared around the side of the house just about the time emotions started to fly.

I took a deep breath, trying to mentally transport myself to the last few days of my parents' life. I didn't remember much, just fuzzy memories of laughter and warm embraces. Even with the eyes of a five-year-old who had yet to discover the intricacies of grown-up love, I couldn't see anything but adoration between my mom and dad.

A sharp prick at my lower leg jerked me back to the present, and I glanced down to find a peppy-looking chicken staring up at me. I pushed away the absurd idea that Rocky Boyd was my father and patted his head. "Hello, Phil."

He made a *gak-gak-gak* noise and pecked at my shin.

"Ow," I said, brushing him away. "That hurt."

Beverlee and Scoots rounded the corner with Ada's next-door neighbor trailing close behind.

"Bud," I said, pointing to the chicken. "Phil is being rude again."

Bud scooped Phil up and gave Beverlee a sheepish grin. "Sorry about that. Phil is a ladies' man. Doesn't like to see a female in distress."

Beverlee fluttered her lashes at him. "That's so sweet. He'd make a great husband."

When her eyes went large, I could almost read the plans running through her brain.

"No," I said, standing up and brushing dirt from the back of my pants. "Don't even think about it."

But she was too far gone. "We're in the middle of an emotional crisis here, Mr. Perkins, but before we take Glory back home, I have to ask you a question. What is your position on arranged marriages?"

He sputtered. "You seem like a lovely woman, Beverlee, but I don't think it's an appropriate time for us to be discussing marriage. We just met."

She swatted him on the shoulder. "Not me, silly. Matilda. I think she'd find Phil utterly charming, and now that she's past egg-laying age, I'd love for her to spend her golden years in the company of a good man." The three of us gaped at her, but she didn't seem to notice. "It's the least she deserves, don't you think?"

~

"I CAN'T BELIEVE you tried to hit on my grandmother's neighbor," I said, pulling the Mustang to a stop in front of the Big River library. "Especially after dropping a bombshell about the chief thinking—erroneously, I might add—that Rocky Boyd was my father."

Beverlee gave me a gentle smile. "I wasn't hitting on him. I was hitting on his chicken."

Scoots pointed at her friend in the rearview mirror. "You are obsessed with marriage. You should have learned your lesson the first four times it didn't work for you."

"Nonsense," Beverlee replied. "There is always room for a new husband. For me, or for my best girl."

It was only slightly annoying that she was referring to her chicken instead of me.

I motioned to the front of the library, a refurbished old house with stately, cream columns and a hedge out front that had been trimmed neatly into a gentle curving pattern on either side of the front door. Unfortunately, the gardener had been a little too overzealous in his trimming. Instead of an elegant row of foliage, the bushes looked like two voluptuous rear ends.

"It has been a long day," I said, stretching my shoulders to relieve the knot of tension that had taken up residence there. "And I still don't understand what we're doing at the library."

"Do you know what the world had before the Internet?" Beverlee asked.

"Peace of mind?"

Beverlee shook her head. "Librarians. The world had librarians. And there is nobody in this town that will be able to give you a better picture of what was happening when Rocky and Daniel fought than Virginia Levi. If you want to prove that your daddy wasn't involved in his brother's death and shut down the rumor that he wasn't even your daddy, then we have to start digging for the truth."

We walked across the lawn, the heat of the day already pressing into our skin. As we pushed open the front door, we were greeted by the smell of old leather and dust, the perfume of libraries for decades.

A young woman in a sundress pushing a cart of books greeted us as we entered the building. "Welcome to the library. I don't think I've seen you here before. Can I help you find something?"

"Is Virginia around?" I asked.

"She's finishing up with story time in the children's section. You might be able to catch her before she gets involved in today's activity—we're reshelving a bunch of books we found in old Mr. Goldthwaite's house. He was a bit of a hoarder, but he was one of our biggest donors."

Scoots leaned in, whispering, "Did he…"

A quick bark of laughter escaped the volunteer's mouth before she clamped her hand over her lips. "Oh no," she replied. "He moved into the assisted living facility down on the waterfront. Apparently, his daughter did not enjoy getting calls from Chief Daly at three in the morning that her dad was wandering through town in his underwear reciting Thoreau at the top of his lungs. Said it scared all the drunk college kids."

Just then, a rush of small children and their coffee cup-toting mothers flooded toward the door. Virginia trailed them across the room, calmly pointing a little boy toward a display of early readers.

When she saw us, her face broke into a wide grin. "I certainly didn't expect to see you here today, Glory. Did something happen with the wedding?"

I assured her everything was on track for both the luncheon and the ceremony.

"I was just telling Glory that librarians are the best resources for gathering information," Beverlee said.

"You're all superheroes who wield plastic protective jackets."

"That's a great compliment." Virginia's posture straightened. Maybe she wasn't used to receiving kind words. She moved to the computer behind the circulation desk. "What can I help you find?"

"I'm trying to put the pieces together about what was happening in town around the time my parents died."

A shadow crossed her face. "I'm not sure how much I can do for you. It was a long time ago. Is there something specific you're looking for?"

I pressed my hand to the desk, swallowing against a lump in my throat. "Do you have any old newspaper articles or anything that might help me get a better picture of what my parents' relationship was like before the accident?"

She nodded once, then led us across the romance section to a door. She tugged a coiled keyring from her wrist and worked at the ancient lock until the door pulled open, finally leading us into a large storage room. It was lined with card catalogs and cardboard boxes, and a rickety wooden table against the far wall held a collection of old machines, including a fax machine that was missing its handset. "It's a mess in here, but if we have anything dating back that far, it will be in here."

"One of these days, I'm going to hire someone to go through everything in this room," she continued, brushing her hands on the front of her pants. "You're welcome to fire up Bessie, our microfiche machine, but she's persnickety even on a good day, and our system for filing old newspaper clippings is less than desirable." She shuffled through a few boxes, pushing them aside until she found what she was seeking. She carried the box across the room to the table, brushing a tape recorder aside and dropping it with a thunk, sending a swirl of dust high into the air. "But I do have something you might find useful. This is everything I kept from high school. There are a few yearbooks and a scrapbook I used to spend hours decorating when Burton and I were first dating."

"Used to?" I asked. "What made you stop?"

"After you're married for a while, it just doesn't seem as necessary to document things," she said, tapping the box top with a fingertip. "Maybe that's one of the reasons I'm so excited about this wedding. It's a fresh start for all of us."

Beverlee murmured in agreement. We all knew the beauty of a new beginning.

A brief wave of sadness crossed through me as I thought of Virginia Levi making the decision to stop putting pictures in her memory book. At what point in a marriage do you give up the idea that the moments are worth capturing?

Scoots peered around me at the box. "Why do you keep your scrapbook here and not at home? That would seem like something you'd want to keep safe."

"That's exactly why it's here. Burton wants to convert our attic into a man cave, and I know I'm going to come home one of these days to a house with a giant hole in the roof." She moved around the room, pointing to a few more boxes. "I believe Warren's baby book is in this one, and over there you'll find my wedding dress and my collection of vintage Nancy Drews."

"That was smart," Beverlee acknowledged. "Men don't always feel as sentimental about our keepsakes as we do."

"I never know what's going to make Burton get emotional. Just last week I caught him getting misty over a baseball glove from when Warren was in Little League. And when they discovered Rocky's body, he spent two solid afternoons pawing through some of these ancient pictures reminiscing about the bygone days and listening to his old cassettes." Virginia waved her hand toward the table and spun toward the door. "Take your time. I'll be at the circulation desk if you need me."

Beverlee flipped the box lid onto the table and offered me a gentle smile. "Are you sure you want to do this? There's nothing wrong with leaving your memories tucked safely away in your heart. If Rocky was your father, do you really want to know?"

Tears stung the corners of my eyes, but I didn't let them fall. "My father, *Daniel Boyd*, wasn't a killer, and if proving his innocence is going to require me to also prove that he was human, so be it." I pulled a yearbook from the box and shoved it across the table toward Scoots. "Start here. We're looking for anything to give us background on what led to the big fight and both of those men losing their lives."

Beverlee grabbed a stack of folded newspapers and took them to an open seat. "This is very retro. I haven't read an actual newspaper in years. Even my blog is fully online now."

My aunt started *Beverlee's Bites* to share recipes and local news, but it had quickly become the town's most frequented gossip website. If it happened in Flat Falls—and sometimes even if it didn't and she just wanted it to—Beverlee put it up on the web.

I gently pulled out Virginia's scrapbook. It was large and bulky, with ribbons and papers peeking out from its overstuffed pages. The cover was made of light pink quilted fabric with a hand-embroidered purple heart sitting slightly off-center.

I ran my finger along the stitching, remembering the times of being young and in love and thinking that every movie ticket and gum wrapper we had shared was worthy of a strip of permanent tape in my memory book.

Even all these years later, I wished I had kept up with

more of what made my relationship with Ian so special. I'd have kept a sugar packet from the cafe where he held my hand for the first time. And maybe a sprig of sea grass from our long walks along the beach or that old ratty sweatshirt he got out of the truck of Scoots's Cadillac and wrapped around my shoulders at the prom.

Instead, I had the ticket stub from the bus I hopped on right after graduation tucked away in a box of memorabilia that also included a copy of the divorce papers my attorney was trying to serve to my disappearing act of an almost-ex-husband.

I felt like a voyeur as I thumbed through the book containing all of Virginia's hopes and dreams for her life with Burton, knowing that down the road he, too, turned out to be a chump.

And he had the look of one, too. In each picture Virginia had so carefully displayed with cut-out frames and colorful stickers, Burton sported a smug grin that said he thought he was better than Big River.

I stopped at a snapshot of young men dressed in tuxedos for their prom. Burton stood in the center, his arm wrapped around Rocky, pulling him forward. The knuckles of his right hand were brushing against his friend's forehead.

Around him, the boys seemed to be laughing. They were probably chuckling at Rocky's humiliation through that rough-and-tumble physicality that teenage boys used to show their affection. Even Wayne Daly, Big River's current police chief, was in on the joke. He stood just on the other side of Rocky, his wide grin displaying braces that reflected the light from the camera flash.

But Rocky wasn't laughing. His cheeks were red, his fists clenched at his side.

"Look," I said, holding the picture up for Beverlee to see. "It seems like Burton was a bully even to his friends."

She nodded. "Maybe Rocky finally had his fill of being pushed around, and he finally confronted Burton."

"And paid the ultimate price for his betrayal," I whispered.

11

———————

We made it back to Flat Falls just in time to see a utility truck hoisting a fifty-foot vinyl banner over the festival entrance. It read: *Condolences, Lucy and Warren.*

Beverlee squinted up at the sign. "Shouldn't that say congratulations?"

"The mayor is feeling very budget-conscious this year," I said, summoning my most diplomatic voice. "He got it on sale, and insisted that if he painted over it, nobody would even notice the difference."

She cocked her head to one side and considered it. "I suppose it might be windy enough that nobody could read the whole sign at once, but it still looks like you're welcoming the whole town to a funeral instead of a wedding."

I jerked both hands up in the air, giving up on diplomacy. "Right? And that's not the worst of it. I tried to talk him out of renting tablecloths from the funeral home, but he wouldn't listen."

Covering her mouth with the tips of her fingers, she

whispered, "He's using funeral linens for his daughter's wedding?"

"Black ones. And when they told him they wouldn't have time to wash them between events, he negotiated to get an additional five percent off to just use the dirty ones. He said you'd never be able to see any stains on the dark fabric." I shuddered. "Lucy offered to pay the difference from her retirement fund just so she could get tablecloths that didn't have morgue juju, but Moe wouldn't hear of it."

I tapped my watch before unlocking the door to the office. "Speaking of which, the bride and groom should be here any minute to go over the last-minute changes to the bridal luncheon."

Beverlee let out a huff and followed me into the lobby of Carolina Weddings. "I still can't believe Moe canceled the catering contract. Shouldn't he be more loyal to the residents of Flat Falls instead of letting that big shot with the even bigger ego ruin your plans?"

I dropped my purse behind the desk and slumped into the leather office chair. "He says he's trying to protect me."

"Protect you?" She scoffed. "From what?"

"He says he's trying to keep my father's name out of the press, but I don't buy it. I think he's trying to protect himself." I reduced my voice to a whisper, even though we were the only people in the office. "If this year's festival isn't a success, the town won't come close to making its budget numbers."

Beverlee dropped a hip onto the corner of the desk, knocking over the candy jar. Instead of cleaning the pieces up, she unwrapped a butter mint and popped it into her mouth. "So? It wouldn't be the first time. He'll just propose a new tax to make up for it."

"Not this time." I shook my head. "Word on the street

is that the town council is going to put up someone to oppose him if he can't turn things around."

"Maybe I'll do it," she suggested, peeling the wrapper off another mint. "This town could use a little shaking up."

I knew better than to dismiss her idea outright, because Beverlee had done plenty of things more outrageous than running for public office. "Moe Fowler has been the mayor of Flat Falls for decades, Beverlee. I don't see him giving up his cushy job without a fight."

The bells on the front door tinkled. Beverlee hopped off the desk and adjusted her cleavage before popping the mint into her mouth with a saucy wink. "I'm always up for a fight."

I tried not to bang my head into the desk as I heard her move toward the door to greet the new arrival.

A moment later, she returned with barely concealed irritation. "The bride and groom have arrived with their entourages in tow, including Burton Levi."

I let out a groan. "How am I supposed to pretend like I don't despise him? He's mean, rude, and potentially a murderer."

She tugged open the top desk drawer and produced a tray of delicate candies wrapped in gold foil. "Help yourself to an emergency chocolate. Cocoa is scientifically proven to make you feel better when you're stressed out."

Beverlee kept a stash of handmade chocolate truffles in her drawer, in her purse, and on her kitchen counter next to the phone in case she got caught by a telemarketer. I had also found them more than once hidden behind the toilet paper underneath her bathroom sink. She said it was because a robber might steal them from the kitchen, but nobody was going to go digging around behind the double-ply expecting a snack.

"If I'm not finished in an hour, come save me," I

instructed, grabbing two chocolates. "Invent a plumbing emergency or something."

She nodded. "You need to have plenty of time to get ready for the festival tonight."

"Honestly, I wasn't planning on going. I have too much left to do for the luncheon."

"Glory Ann Wells," she said, propping a fist on her hip. "You can't live in Flat Falls and miss the official opening night at the Roadkill Jubilee. It's just not done."

"Josie can't go," I said, searching for excuses. "So I thought I'd just hang out at home and keep her company."

"*Josie* is incarcerated in her living room. That's a valid reason to skip the social event of the year. *You* are just hiding from Ian."

I opened my mouth to argue, but then snapped my teeth closed because she was mostly correct. Since I'd moved back to Flat Falls, I had spent equal amounts of time searching the streets for him and hiding behind bushes if I spotted him in town.

I inhaled slowly and pointed toward the door. "I'm going to work now."

"Have fun." She waggled her fingers in the air. "And don't forget to play nice with the murderer. You don't want to end up buried beneath the new statue before you get a chance to clear your father's name."

I ROUNDED the corner to the conference room where the Fowler family sat positioned on one side of the table with the Levi family on the other. Nobody was speaking, and from the ruddiness of Burton's cheeks, he was moments away from throwing a meaty punch.

He pushed back when he saw me, the chair scraping

against the stained cement floor. "You kept us waiting long enough."

"My apologies, Mr. Levi," I said with a falsely cheerful voice. "I'm sure you of all people can understand how hectic it can get as an event gets closer. Tomorrow will be here before we know it, and I wanted to make sure we have everything in place for the luncheon."

Neither Ruby nor Warren returned my greeting. They were too busy avoiding eye contact with each other. Ruby fidgeted with her engagement ring, while Warren studied his reflection in the mirrored lamp that sat on the sideboard beside the conference room table.

It was never a good sign when the bride and groom pretended not to know each other in the days leading up to the wedding.

"Warren, I'm glad you're finally able to join us. Ruby has been telling me how hard you've been working lately and how proud she is of you."

He looked up in surprise. "She has?"

My eyes flashed to Ruby, who had lifted a brow as if asking me where I had come up with that. In truth, she had been telling me how busy her fiancé was, but it was mostly in the context of how she wouldn't even recognize him at the altar because it had been so long since she'd seen his face.

"Yes, of course," I replied with a patient smile. "And Ruby, Warren is going to pass out when he sees you in that gown." I leaned toward him with a conspiratorial whisper. "You're going to be the envy of every man on the coast. She's a knockout."

Ruby flushed, and Warren flashed a look of appreciation toward her. "I'm a lucky man."

And that was all it took for the lovebirds to scoot their chairs next to each other, the stress of wedding planning and running around with scandalous women already forgotten.

"So, let's just confirm we've got everything ready for tomorrow," I said, whipping out my portfolio and spreading the multi-page checklist on the table in front of me. "Warren, I'm glad to see that you'll be joining us for the luncheon."

He shifted in his chair and cleared his throat. "Well, um… actually… I'm heading out tonight. Ruby can handle finger sandwiches and opening presents on her own."

"Finger sandwiches?" Burton's voice boomed from across the room. "Is that what you think of me, son?"

I held my hand out to stop him from talking. "We'll get to the menu in a moment. Ruby, are you okay with going to the luncheon without your fiancé?"

Virginia sent a tired look toward her husband before placing a hand on Warren's arm. "Boys will be boys, I'm afraid. But we'll all be there to celebrate with you, Ruby."

"Back in my day, bridal lunches were for the bride." Burton scrunched up his nose as if the word *bride* smelled like rotten Brussels sprouts. "My boy is doing what all the men before him have done and not apologized for. He's having one last taste of freedom before he gets the ol' ball and chain."

Ruby blanched, and metal chair legs scraped against the floor as both Totty and Moe scooted closer to their daughter. She gathered her composure and brushed them off. "It's fine. It's going to be a beautiful day."

I took that single moment of optimism and ran with it. If the bride was pretending it was okay for her groom to be off at a floating kegger instead of by her side at their party, who was I to argue?

"Now that we've confirmed the guest list, can we take a

quick look at the menu?" I asked. "It seems to have gotten away from me when Lavish took the contract."

I still fumed when I remembered the look on Ian's face when Moe cancelled the contract. For years, the mayor had talked about the importance of supporting local businesses, but when it came time for him to actually do it, he caved in the name of politics.

Burton thrust his pointer finger toward me. "You don't need to worry about it. We've got it under control."

"I have no doubt about that, but it sure would be helpful if you let me in on the plan so I can make sure the event flows smoothly. We want to feature your dishes appropriately, and I'll need to have time to set up the appropriate… lighting."

I tried not to roll my eyes at my own blubbering. From what Ian had said, Burton managed his kitchen like a boot camp with extra sharp knives. He wouldn't be convinced to turn over the menu just because I offered him a lamp.

"Lighting," he acknowledged with a snap. "Always an important part of showcasing culinary art." He regarded me for a moment before turning his finger toward his wife. "You heard her. Make sure Oliver sends over the full menu tonight."

Virginia gave him a blank stare. "But Oliver is gone."

He slammed his palm on the table with such sudden force that we all jumped. "Then get him back, just like you always do."

A shiver skated down my spine as I watched his body tense and release.

He was certainly capable of violence, but had Burton really killed his best friend?

~

AFTER THE SUN went down that night, my craving for a powdered sugar-covered funnel cake outweighed my desire to lounge around in my pajamas playing with the only food I had in my apartment, which included wilted kale and a basket of sugar packets. The kale was a gift from Beverlee's garden, and it taunted me from the bare refrigerator shelves until it finally gave up from being ignored and fainted into a floppy pile. Just like Beverlee when she didn't get enough attention.

The sugar I had pilfered from the Grind and Go the last time I got a latte.

As I approached the festival center, the air was heavy with the scent of corn dogs and fried dough, and the bright lights of the food carts and carnival games reflected off the water. My stomach grumbling, I stopped to stare up at an enormous rack of roasted turkey legs, their juices dripping as they turned slowly above a flame. Since a giant stick of roasted meat sounded like a good base for the rest of the junk food I planned to indulge in, I took a step forward, eager to get the vendor's attention.

Suddenly, I felt a hand clamp over my shoulder. "I wouldn't do that. They have a setup behind the scenes that would give the health inspector a coronary."

I whirled around to see Oliver French, Burton's recently fired assistant chef. "Thanks for the warning." I grabbed my stomach and grimaced. "There's nothing worse than the regret you feel the morning after rancid carnival food."

He grinned and took a bow. "I'm a hero to many."

I couldn't help but laugh. Despite working for a world-class jerk like Burton Levi, Oliver kept a sense of humor, and that was an attractive trait in a man. I glanced around and lowered my voice. "Sorry about the other day. I didn't mean for the luncheon plans to get you fired."

"Don't worry about that," he said, waving his hand in

front of my forehead as if trying to wipe my memory. "He does that sometimes."

"He fires you? Regularly?"

"Yes. But then he realizes he actually needs me, so he gives me a raise and promises to never do it again."

"That sounds terrible." I felt bad for all of Burton's employees who had to deal with his explosive temper every day.

"What doesn't kill you makes you…"

I piped in with a response. "Stronger?"

"No. Richer." He put his hand back on my shoulder and ushered me out of the walkway. "Burton sent me a text earlier and said you needed a copy of the menu for tomorrow. I can drop one by your office. Or if you want to give me your number, I'll send it over electronically."

I pulled my wallet from my pocket and fished out a business card, brushing my finger over its crinkled edge just enough to make it flutter to the ground. When it landed on the toe of a brown leather work boot that didn't belong to the loafered man in front of me, I jerked my head up.

"Ian," I said, my voice far more breathless than I would have liked for it to be. "I didn't see you standing there."

He angled a brow toward Oliver. "Obviously."

The two squared off to face each other, shoulders pulled back.

"Ian," Oliver said with a stiff nod.

I could sense the tension crackling in the summer air with an electricity more intense than the flashing neon sign at the turkey cart, so I did what I always do when faced with an uncomfortable situation where I'm sandwiched between two handsome men: I babbled.

"Oh, you know each other!" I shrieked with high-pitched faux delight. "Isn't the weather lovely tonight? Oliver and I were just talking about carnival food, and I can't decide whether to get an ice cream cone or a chocolate-dipped—"

Ian reached out and gave my arm a gentle squeeze. "Oliver and I go way back. We worked together at Burton's restaurant."

"It's true," Oliver replied. "We once shared a lovely bottle of vintage bourbon after Burton fired us on the same night."

"But he didn't hire me back," Ian mused.

Oliver acknowledged that with a nod, then pointed toward the tent where the luncheon would be held. "Sorry about the catering job, but you know how he is."

"If I was worrying about the food for tomorrow, I wouldn't be able to come to the festival at all." Ian dropped his hand to intertwine with mine. "And then I would have missed the chance to spend the evening with one of my favorite people."

I ignored the urge to check over my shoulder to see who else he could have been talking about. I had broken his heart once upon a time, and I didn't think that qualified me for all-star company status.

Instead of waiting for my answer, Ian tugged on my hand. "So we'll be seeing you later, Oliver."

Oliver may have grunted, or he may have spontaneously combusted into a flurry of miniature dragons. Either way, I wouldn't have noticed.

Instead, I let Ian lead me down toward the waterfront, only gathering my senses when he lingered in front of the rickety Ferris wheel.

I whirled toward him. "Number one: what was that about? You don't get to just grab me and drag me away when I'm talking to another man."

"And number two?" he asked, the pad of his thumb still caressing my palm.

I pointed to the Ferris wheel. "Nope."

He flashed me a lopsided grin, and I felt proud of myself for standing firm instead of shuffling my feet and letting the blush that was threatening to creep up my cheeks take over. I wiggled my hand free. "Your dimple magic won't work this time."

"Okay, first of all, Oliver isn't the nice guy you think he is. Burton keeps him around because he needs someone to do his dirty work."

"That Oliver? He's perfectly nice. I can't even imagine where you'd get the idea that he's some sort of bad—"

Ian's gaze darkened. "He's responsible for Belinda Grant's restaurant going out of business."

My jaw dropped. The Crab Palace had been a fixture around Flat Falls for years, and Belinda's recipe for cracker-breaded soft-shell crabs had been the reason. My mouth watered just thinking about them. "I wondered what happened to that place."

Ian and I had spent many Saturday evenings crowded in a corner booth at the waterfront restaurant. Belinda had a tender spot for him and always piled our plates much higher than our teenage budget would allow.

"The crab harvest was a bust a few years ago," Ian said. "Too many hurricanes and too much boat traffic. But the fishermen that were left were loyal to Belinda. She had treated them well for years and often overpaid what the crop was worth just so they'd be able to stick around. When Burton found out there wouldn't be enough crabs to supply both restaurants, he sent Oliver in to convince Belinda to take them off her menu so he could serve them to his hoity-toity, white-glove patrons."

"But she didn't, right?"

Belinda had never been a pushover. She ruled her

kitchen with a kind, but firm hand. She was fair and honest, and all her employees respected her work ethic.

"No, she didn't," he said sadly. "The restaurant had been struggling enough as it was. Removing them from her menu would have meant the end of The Crab Palace." He shifted. "When he couldn't get her to back down, Burton sent Oliver in to negotiate with the fishermen. He doubled the price Belinda could pay, and he threatened to pull the whole contract if they did business with her anymore."

"Oh, no. Crabs were her livelihood. Without them…"

"She went under in less than six weeks."

"Did you know what was happening?" I asked.

He shook his head. "Not until the For Sale sign went up on the building. And by then it was too late. She had already moved to Ohio."

I was still contemplating the unfairness of Belinda losing her beloved restaurant when Ian nudged me forward to the platform.

The carnival worker slowed the seat to a gentle swing and motioned for us to get on.

"Come on. I promise I'll take care of you."

I leaned forward and whispered, "It is a whirling death cage that gets wheeled around from town to town and rebuilt every week. I'm sure it's held together with rusty screws and plastic cable ties."

"Ma'am, there's no need to be nervous," the ride operator said, pointing to the line of people that had formed behind us. "See? Even the little ones like it."

Taking a step backward, I barely missed a toddler clutching a teddy bear and patiently waiting for his turn. "I don't think…"

A bubbly sound came spewing forth from the back of Ian's throat.

"No," I said, fighting a combination of laughter and

mortification. "Don't start. You know how much I hate the—"

Ian clucked. He stuck his hands under his armpits and bent his knees, bouncing around on the platform as he channeled his inner chicken.

Matilda would have been proud.

And my guess is she would have wanted Ian more than she wanted Phil.

Understandably.

Ian finally stopped making noise and pressed his mouth to my ear. "You don't have to. But I've been dying to get you alone, and sitting on top of the world with you for five minutes sounds like an outstanding way to spend an evening."

Moments later, I found my feet swinging freely as the salty sea air brushed against my skin.

"I can't believe you talked me into this," I said.

He slipped his arm around my shoulder. "You never were a chicken."

And he was right. Once upon a time, I would have been the first person in line for the Ferris wheel. Now, as I white-knuckled the safety bar, I willed seventeen-year-old Glory to climb back into my body.

She wouldn't have her eyes squeezed shut to avoid looking down. She wouldn't be fighting to keep down the protein bar she'd eaten hours before. No, she'd be cheering and hollering, both hands stuck up in the air, as she took in the beautiful waterfront and the handsome man locked into place beside her. She'd probably say something witty and make a move on him.

"Easy," Ian said, the feel of his hand over mine dragging me back to the present. "You're looking a bit green around the edges. Just take a few deep breaths. It will come back to you."

I followed his instruction and slowly inhaled through my nose to the count of five. Beverlee called it meditative breathing, and she swore it cured stress and made her look half her age.

I popped one eye open, not ready to acknowledge that she might have been onto something.

"Stay with me," Ian said, his voice calm and kind.

I managed to summon a smile, opening my eyes and taking in the crowd below. The Roadkill Jubilee was always a menagerie of colors and flavors, but to see it from the sky brought a whole new appreciation to the festival our little town had created. "It's really beautiful up here, once you look past the cotter pin that's holding this rickety thing together."

He laughed. "That's my girl."

My heart flopped over like a rainbow trout caught in a fishing net, but instead of overanalyzing what he meant by those three words, I pointed down at the food truck with flashing orange and yellow signs that advertised fresh falafel. "I know where my first stop is going to be when we get back to safe ground."

He nodded approvingly. "At least you're not choosing one of those grotesque turkey legs."

"Me?" I pressed a finger to the center of my chest. "Never."

The movement of the ride slowed, and we came to a swinging stop at the top. "We can see the ocean from up here," Ian said.

"And Flat Falls looks so small." I leaned forward until the seat squeaked, and then I made a matching noise and settled back against Ian's arm. "And there's Carolina Weddings. I wish we could see the front of the building. I'll bet it looks extra sparkly tonight."

Beverlee and I had spent hours stringing twinkle lights

along the front glass windows, giving the shop a magical glow. But instead of the festive lighting, we had a prime view of the back entrance that shared an alley with the pawnshop and my apartment.

Just as the Ferris wheel jerked and started moving again, I saw a dark shadow emerge from the window at the back of my office. "Ian, there's somebody—"

The wheel slammed to a stop again, but this time we were in a lower position. "I can't see," I shrieked, slamming my hand into the metal bar that held us in. "Somebody was in there."

Ian craned his neck. "I don't see anything. Are you sure—"

"Let us down!" I screamed down to the ride worker. "Hurry!"

But he couldn't hear us. And instead of bringing us to a halt at the bottom of the ride, he gave us a spirited wave and sent us spinning up into the air again.

I was helpless, trapped at the top of the world, watching from above as somebody broke into my office.

12

Ian called the police as I hyperventilated on the Ferris wheel, and by the time we elbowed through the crowd toward Carolina Weddings, Hollis and his detective, Gage Russell, were waiting for us.

"Did you catch him?" I asked, dragging in breaths as I sprinted up to the building.

Hollis shook his head, motioning for me to unlock the door. "No, but the back window is broken. Somebody definitely tried to get inside. Probably a rabble-rouser from the festival. I'm going to need you to give me an inventory of the things that were stolen so we can put a notice out to all the pawnshops in the area."

My stomach dropped. I was just getting Carolina Weddings off the ground, and the thought of someone running off with my computer equipment or any of the wedding props we kept in the storage closet made my fists clench.

I slid my key into the lock, taking a deep breath before I pushed it open.

The door's entry bell tinkled above my head, and I reached up to silence it as I scanned the room.

From the front door, nothing looked disturbed. Beverlee's laptop sat folded closed on the reception desk next to a vase stuffed with Gerbera daisies from her garden.

I shuffled through the office, noting that the conference table was immaculate, and the supply closet door was still closed.

Just then, Beverlee pushed past the police chief and gathered me in her arms. "I came as soon as I heard."

"But… how?" I asked, my voice muffled against her linen jumpsuit, a jaunty buffalo plaid number with blue and white checks that tied with two pieces of rope around the back of her neck.

She offered me a puzzled look. "Shirley called me."

Of course Shirley had called her. She had a prime view of the flashing blue lights from the vantage point of the Grind and Go.

But if it hadn't been Shirley, someone else would have started the Flat Falls gossip party line. No errant behavior ever went unnoticed, and while that usually annoyed me, I felt strangely comforted by my aunt's quick arrival and the small crowd of nosy neighbors clustered outside the door.

"Is anything missing?" Beverlee asked.

I stepped into my office, expecting to see it trashed. But nothing seemed amiss. It was still messy, but not burglar messy. Just ordinary, everyday messy.

"No," I said slowly, dropping an empty paper coffee cup into the trash and trying to will my hands to stop shaking. "It looks like everything is here."

"Maybe it would be easier to tell if you'd actually pick up in here occasionally," Beverlee muttered under her breath. "It's like your grandmother used to say, 'You should wear clean underwear in case you get into an accident, and always leave your desk tidy when you leave for the day.'"

I crinkled my brow. "In case you get robbed?"

"Exactly!" she replied, apparently satisfied that I understood the importance of tidiness if faced with either bodily injury or intruders.

I turned to Hollis, who was directing Gage to clean up the broken glass from the back window. "Seems like you got here just in time. I can't see that anything is missing, and I'm sure insurance will cover the window."

"Gage is going to board it up for you, just in case there's rain," Hollis replied. "And if you do notice anything amiss, you know where to find—"

My gasp interrupted him. "My box. It's gone," I said, pointing to the side of my desk where the dusty cardboard box had rested. "Somebody stole the box my grandmother gave me— The one that was going to help me clear my father's name."

AFTER WE CLEANED up the glass and ensured that the office was locked up tight, Ian headed off to work and Beverlee and I wandered back down to the waterfront. This time, despite the upbeat music and the promise of a fresh apple fritter, my heart wasn't into it. The last few days hadn't been kind to my emotional well-being, and none of the treats Beverlee offered helped to raise my spirits.

"I just don't understand," I said. "Is this some kind of cruel joke? First, I find another body, then somebody spreads horrible lies about my father, and now I've been robbed? And what kind of idiot would break into a building just to steal a box of old photographs and a broken baseball trophy?"

She lifted a brow.

I brushed her aside, remembering several times we had slipped into buildings without permission. "Besides us, I mean. And we usually have a very good reason."

"What if the burglar did, too? I'll bet there was something in that box that would incriminate him in Rocky's murder."

"Like what?" I asked. "It was a bunch of sentimental junk an old lady kept around to remember her dead son."

Sons, I reminded myself. Ada Boyd lost two boys, one after the other. And even though I wasn't a fan of my grandmother, not knowing what happened to one of them must have been gut-wrenching.

When we stopped in front of a street musician playing an old Beach Boys song, Beverlee dug into the front of her blouse and produced a dollar bill. She tossed it into his open guitar case, wiggling her shoulders dramatically to the music. She twirled and bounced as the music reached a crescendo, seemingly unaware of the catcalls from passersby.

At least two people had their cell phone cameras out, filming the whole thing. She gifted them with a wink before giving a flirty bow and brushing past me. "You're right," she said, ignoring the small crowd her impromptu dance had drawn. "Thirty-year-old prom pictures don't exactly scream, 'motive.'"

I studied her for a moment, then turned back to the group, who had begun to disperse. "But what if they do?"

She paused, her hand on her hip. "What do you mean?"

"Most people aren't as free-spirited as you, right?"

She acknowledged that with a shrug. "Maybe not. But they should be. People spend far too much time caring about what other people think instead of living for themselves. If they would just get those sticks out of their—"

"But twenty years from now," I interrupted, "when the videos of you dancing like that resurface, are you going to feel the same way?"

"Yes," she replied with a shimmy. "Of course. I have a nice rack, and I'm sure I will look back on it fondly."

"Your… um… assets aside, though." I fought the urge to wrap my arms around her waist to prevent her from flitting around like a half-drunk butterfly. "What if you were doing something you'd be embarrassed about?"

"Such as?" She wrinkled her brow as if she'd never considered the idea that her behavior would ever be embarrassing.

Which was probably true. Not much fazed her, and she lived her history proudly. She even showed off pictures of the bad perm she got in the eighties that turned her hair an odd shade of green and made her look like a piece of yard waste that had gotten momentarily electrocuted.

"Making eyes at your best friend's girlfriend," I suggested.

She stared off into space, flipping through her mental Rolodex. For a woman who couldn't remember to lock her front door half the time, she had a mind built for recalling the most minute detail about someone else's life. She called it being neighborly, but the rest of us just called it nosy. "The box didn't contain anything incriminating, though. Just some old pictures."

"There were several pictures of Rocky with Burton and Virginia," I said. "And one of them must have been proof that Rocky was having an affair with her."

"So you think…"

"I think Burton Levi broke into my office to steal the evidence that his wife was cheating on him with his best friend." My heart thumped along with the distant sound of music. "Evidence that proves his motive in Rocky's death."

~

AFTER ALL THE EXCITEMENT, Beverlee and I decided we needed a snack to help clear our heads, my appetite rising along with my suspicions that my groom's father was a killer.

The lines at the other food trucks were long, so we found ourselves in front of the breakfast truck for the second time that day.

I studied the menu. "I think I'm going to have the bacon special. It has a woven bacon shell, with scrambled eggs, cheese, and more bacon."

"If you have a heart attack, I'm going to leave you right here on the sidewalk as a reminder to everyone about how important it is to eat your vegetables."

I gave her a dramatic sigh and turned to the counter to place my order. "I'll have the Big Bacon, please."

Beverlee cleared her throat.

"Fine," I said with a resigned sigh. "And can you add jalapeños?"

"Make that two," Beverlee said, sidling up to next to me.

Just as I was about to pull out my wallet to pay for our order, I noticed a couple standing off to the side of the festivities, almost hidden beneath the gnarled branches of a live oak tree. Their heads were bowed close together as if they shared a secret they were keeping from the rest of the world.

I thought it looked sweet and romantic until the man raised his head, his face illuminated by the twinkle lights strung through the branches above.

I nudged my chin into the air, motioning for Beverlee to check out the couple. "Looks like Oliver-the-chef found himself a little appetizer." I craned my neck to get a better glimpse of Oliver's female companion. "Wait… is that Virginia?"

Beverlee reached into her pocket and extracted a pair of yellow glasses that glittered with sparkly rhinestones. After slipping them on, she made a clicking sound with her tongue. "I wonder if Burton realizes his wife is getting friendly with his assistant. That would give him a real reason to fire Oliver."

"Wow, for being as strait-laced as she is, that woman does seem to keep a string of admirers," I noted.

When Virginia ducked out from underneath Oliver's arm and started toward us, I grabbed Beverlee's arm. "We can't let her see us," I whispered, whipping my head around to find somewhere to hide.

"In there," Beverlee said, shoving me through the food truck's unlocked back door.

She pulled the door closed behind me, leaving me face-first on a slick black mat that smelled like cat food and ham.

I pushed myself up to my hands and knees, stopping when I came face-to-calf with a pair of grimy boots. I lifted my hand as I struggled to my feet. "This is a really nice truck you've got here. One of our favorites. And we were really hoping you could give us a tour."

The owner scowled and stared me down, while I stood there with a dorky grin pretending to have an abnormal interest in the flat top grill behind her.

Grease dripped from the surface into a bucket below, and off to the side, a fryer fizzed and bubbled with thick slabs of bacon. It wouldn't take much for her to slide out that fryer basket and clock me with it, and from the way she was glaring at me, I suspected the thought had crossed her mind.

But instead of knocking me out with the basket of fiery processed meat, she yanked it out of the fryer and set it to drain in one motion before selecting two eggs and cracking them, one-handed, onto the flat top. She grabbed a long metal spatula and chopped the eggs, the clanging of metal echoing through the truck's interior.

Finally, she turned to me, crossing one arm over her chest and using the spatula in her other hand as a pointer, which she directed toward my stomach with a sneer. "Are you sure you're not the health inspector?"

Although I considered health inspectors noble professionals that kept me from dying from dysentery, her tone suggested they were monsters who chopped up baby goats for fun.

I backed up under her intense gaze until I was pressed against the door, its metal cold against my back. I shook my head back and forth so quickly that it made me dizzy. "No," I replied. "I'm just a big fan of breakfast."

She continued to study me for a moment before her face broke into a smile, highlighting a sparkling gold crown on one of her front canine teeth. Finally satisfied I wasn't there to enforce health regulations, she scooped the eggs off the griddle and folded them into a basket lined with waxed paper. "Breakfast is under-appreciated. It's the best meal of the day."

I agreed with a brisk nod, sliding my hand along the door until my fingers brushed up against the handle. I was about to make a quick escape when the chef spoke the magic words no civil human had ever been able to resist: "Do you like waffle cake?"

My stomach propelled me forward before my brain had a chance to chime in. "I like waffles. And cake," I responded, my voice eager despite my brush with fear just moments earlier.

She hooked her foot around a stool and slid it out from under the counter, inviting me to take a seat.

She introduced herself as Masha and spent the next half hour whipping up homemade waffles, which she cooked until they were crispy, then layered them with thick caramel sauce she made from sweetened condensed milk. Masha kept working until she had a stack that was six inches tall, then she stuck a cutting board on top and smashed it down until the sauce was oozing down the plate.

"Here," she said, tossing a fork on the plate and thrusting the confection toward me. She watched with narrowed eyes as I took a hesitant bite.

For a moment, I wondered if she had poisoned me, believing I was an undercover inspector bent on writing her up for the gross layer of residue that coated most of the surfaces in the back of the truck. But the moment the caramel hit my taste buds, I decided it didn't matter. If I was going to get murdered in the middle of a crowded street on a random spring night, I wanted Masha's waffle cake to be the implement of my demise.

"Masha," I crooned, wiping my mouth with my sleeve before diving in for a second bite. "This is amazing. Where have you been all my life?"

"Big River."

That explained why I had never seen her at the Roadkill Jubilee before. It also gave me an idea. If anyone had the scoop on the Levi family's food empire and their predilection for murder, it would be a nonchalant business owner whose grease-covered food truck could slip in and out of events unnoticed.

She snatched a fork from the drying rack next to the sink, then swiped a bite of a waffle cake from my plate. I couldn't figure out a way to snatch the plate away from her without seeming rude, so I pushed it toward her. If I shared my food, maybe she would share information.

"So, how are things over in Big River?" I asked. "Anything interesting happen in, say, the last twenty-five years?"

She speared a bite of waffle roughly the size of a deck of poker cards and shoved it in her mouth, mumbling as crumbs tumbled down onto her apron. "What do you want to know?"

"Well, I'm a wedding planner, and I'm in charge of the ceremony for someone you might recognize."

"Who?" she asked, grabbing the bowl of caramel and swiping through it with one finger.

She offered it to me, but I shook my head. I would do a lot of things for dessert, but I didn't know where that woman's hands had been. At least she used clean spoons for the cake. "Warren Levi. You might know his father—"

"Burton Levi," she spat, his name evidently less palatable than the rancid oil left over after a batch of bacon had been burned beyond saving.

"Yes, that's him. Do you know him?"

Her gaze darkened, and she seized the plate away from me, dumping the remaining cake in the trash. "No. I've never heard of him."

I stared at the trash can, loss rolling through the space in my stomach left untouched by Masha's cake. "But you just said—"

"I didn't say anything," Masha responded, pushing past me to the back of the truck. She threw the door open, letting a blast of fresh air punch through the truck. "And the tour's over."

"But..."

She pointed out the back, her expression suddenly menacing. "Go."

As I merged into the crowd, I looked back over my

shoulder to find Masha watching me. She stepped back into the truck and closed the door, leaving me standing in the middle of the street wondering what Burton Levi had done to make her hate him enough to throw away a perfectly good cake.

13

On the morning of the luncheon, Beverlee met me at the Grind and Go early enough that the mist was rising over the waterfront and most of the tourists were still lounging in their high-priced hotel beds.

"Where did you go after you shoved me into the food truck?" I motioned for the barista to add a second blueberry muffin to my bag.

Beverlee glanced down sheepishly. "Sorry about that. I ran into Hollis and asked him about the plans for investigating your office break-in. He invited me for ice cream, and before I knew it, it was midnight. I went back to the food truck to look for you, but it was dark. I didn't hear you screaming from inside, so I figured you were probably already gone."

"Probably? What if she had killed me and left me to die in a pile of bacon on her greasy floor?"

She shrugged. "There are worse ways to go, I suppose."

I glared at her. "I can't believe you went on an ice cream date while I was being murdered."

"First of all, it wasn't a date. We were discussing your

case." She raked her gaze down my body. "And second, you don't look murdered. You'd be a lot paler if you were dead."

I pushed open the exterior door, not even bothering to hold it open for her. She shuffled behind me. "Fine, I'm sorry. I saw Virginia coming our way, and I did the first thing that popped into my head. And then I felt so bad about it that I had to get some ice cream."

I shook my head. There was no doubt that Beverlee would go to the ends of the earth for me, even though she'd stop for a snack on the way.

"It's all right," I said. "Masha was actually pretty nice. And she even made me cake."

Beverlee's eyes brightened.

"Oddly enough, she pretended to not know Burton when I asked her about him."

"I would wager there are a lot of people who would prefer to not know Burton," she replied, nodding toward the side of the tent, where a shiny black truck with the Lavish logo blocked multiple lanes of traffic.

Burton's employees scurried to unload food boxes from the back of the truck, carrying them to the custom-built kitchen tent tacked on to the rear of the main tent.

Burton stood in the center wearing a crisp white apron, scowling as he barked orders. "No!" he shouted at a young man unloading cardboard boxes wrapped in plastic. "Do you not understand the meaning of the words 'temperature controlled'? That means you need to run. Don't walk, don't saunter, don't stroll. Run!"

The man took off at an impressive pace, his head ducked like he was making a dash for the end zone with the game-winning ball tucked under his arm.

"Good morning," I said as we approached Burton. "You're up early."

"I would have been here earlier if these idiots would do their jobs."

While he glowered at the crew who scrambled around responding to his demands, I practiced my mental yoga. I had never done actual yoga before, but I imagined myself stretched out flat on the beach with a fruity drink in my hand, taking long, cleansing breaths, and I figured it was pretty close.

Once my blood pressure ventured back down toward normal, I squared my shoulders and followed one of Burton's minions into the tent, not sure what Beverlee and I were in for.

Usually, at this point in the wedding preparations, I had a firm grip on what was happening. I had the last few days before a wedding mapped down to the minute, knowing exactly what time each vendor was arriving and what they were doing.

But this time, I was flying without radar or a map. Burton had not only commandeered the menu for the bridal luncheon, but he had also threatened the florist with legal action for choosing wildflowers for the centerpieces and intentionally knocked over the balloon arch she had hand-built to surround the dessert table.

She was in tears when she called me first thing that morning, and I suspected by the end of the day, the rest of us would be, too.

I spotted her hunkered down in a corner, piles of pink peonies surrounding her like a floral fortress. Her eyes darted toward Beverlee in a panic when she caught our movement but quickly shone with relief when she realized we weren't there to chop her up with a carving knife.

I waved, then whispered to Beverlee, "If you can handle the flower crisis, I'll get Burton under control." I said it with a lot more confidence than I felt. There wasn't enough armor in the world to prepare myself for battle with the beast of a human that was Burton Levi.

But I was determined to keep Lucy's bridal luncheon from erupting into a bloodbath, so I swallowed my fear and marched up to Burton. "I'm looking forward to seeing what culinary magic you cook up to…aah!"

Before he could respond, I tripped over a power cable and fell to the floor at his feet. The sheer humiliation, combined with his disgusted glare, caused me to break down in a fit of giggles. By the time I gathered my wits, my mascara was smeared, and I had a raging case of hiccups.

Burton leveled a hard gaze at me, probably wishing for a sinkhole to open and swallow me whole. When it didn't, he pointed toward the large ceramic grill that was being rolled across the floor on a dolly. "Are you quite through? I have tenderloins to prepare, and I don't have time to sit here all morning watching you lose your mind like your father."

My breath caught in my throat. "My… father?"

"I hope foul temperaments and irrational conduct are not hereditary. My team has more than enough to do today without having to manage another member of the Boyd family whose senses have gone amiss."

According to Beverlee, there were a few things I had gotten from my father. His brown hair. His love for singing show tunes obnoxiously loud in the shower.

And finally, his temper.

With my fists clenched at my side, I lurched forward. "I don't know who you think you are, Mr. Levi, but if you had any sort of history with my father, you'd know that he was a good man who…"

"Murdered his brother?" His cheeks reddened, and spittle gathered at the corners of his lips.

I felt the screech building in my chest before it flew out of my mouth, accompanied by a curse so foul I could almost taste the soap Beverlee would have used to scrub out my mouth for using it.

Burton's lips pursed, and he stepped back with an appraising glance that held none of the rancor he had spewed just moments before. "I take that back. You're more like your mother."

He said it as if it was a good thing, and his sudden shift to pleasantries caught me by surprise.

I took a step back, the fire in my chest retreating as if doused with a glass of ice water. "You knew my mom?"

"Of course. Everybody knew Lucy," he responded, giving an uncharacteristic chuckle. "And probably half the town was in love with her."

I had always heard my mother left a trail of broken hearts behind her, but Beverlee said that once she met my father, she never looked at another man.

We had been sharing a deep-dish pizza she had specially ordered to heal my broken teenage heart when a boy from my homeroom asked another girl to the Homecoming dance. I asked her if I'd ever find true love. In true Beverlee fashion, she had answered, "Yes, baby. And if you're like me, maybe more than once." Then she stretched a string of melted mozzarella to her lips and related my parents' love story for the hundredth time. "Or you could be like your mom and dad. Once Lucy met Daniel, that was it for her. Nobody else existed."

I remembered that about them. They'd sit on the front porch swing, her head resting on his chest and his fingers swirling on the skin of her bare shoulders.

Sometimes, she'd fall asleep, and he'd motion for me to grab the old afghan off the sofa so he could wrap it around her. And then he would just hold her while she slept.

There was no way she would have looked twice at Rocky Boyd; she only had eyes for one man. My father.

I dragged my attention back to Burton, who was flipping through an invoice.

"You were my uncle's best friend, and you were there the night they fought," I said. "Do you know what they were fighting about?"

He hesitated and then glanced back at me over his shoulder. "Whom."

"I'm confused."

"Don't be dense." Dismissing me with a wave, he moved toward the temporary kitchen, where a portable refrigeration trailer was being assembled. "The important thing isn't what they were fighting about. It's whom. And that's the big question, isn't it?"

I tried to get more details before he disappeared into the trailer, but he was already lost in the sea of cocktail shrimp and petit fours.

~

I SHOULD HAVE REALIZED the morning's abrupt start was going to set the tone for the day when the Methodist Ladies Book Club showed up two hours early for the luncheon.

I met them at the tent's entrance and tried to shoo them back outside, but they were a persistent bunch.

"Ladies." I addressed the small crowd who had gathered in their Saturday finest, which today included a variety of floral dresses that could have doubled as upholstery fabric. "You look lovely today, and we're delighted to have you join us for the celebration of Ruby and Warren's wedding—but, unfortunately, we're not ready to welcome guests."

A woman I didn't recognize, probably because she was wearing a large floppy hat that measured two feet across and obscured most of her features, stepped forward. "We won't be any bother, dear. We just wanted to get a good seat. And Magnolia told us you might need some extra help." And with that, they dispersed like a gaggle of busybody toddlers, spreading to the far corners of the tent.

Leave it to Maggie to curse me from the other side of town. She was probably laughing into her bubbling cauldron as she pictured ruining more of my wedding plans.

I quickly found Beverlee, who was trying to cover an unrecognizable stain on the top of the table linens. When I leaned over to get her attention, my hand pressed into something sticky.

"Please tell me the wetness is spot remover because I can't handle thinking about why the funeral parlor sent over tablecloths soaked with dead people goo," I whispered, pinching my nose and choking back a gag. "That smells like Gruyère."

Beverlee spritzed the stain with cleanser and started scrubbing. "Trigger Lee Wagner's wake was last night," she said with a nod. "And what started as a friendly gathering of a few friends turned into an all-night keg party with a barbecue trailer and a fondue station. People came from two counties over."

I couldn't imagine that many people showing up for my funeral.

Beverlee, on the other hand, had already purchased a burial plot in the center of the only cemetery in Flat Falls that got enough foot traffic so she wouldn't be lonely. She had also signed a catering contract, hired a mariachi band, and purchased a dress for the occasion. It was a bright red number with a flouncy skirt and a form-fitting halter top so she could make her march to eternity without needing a bra.

She had even stitched a message on a pillow to remind me: *Nobody wants to spend their afterlife being poked by an underwire.*

Even though I reminded her she was nowhere near needing a funeral, Beverlee said she wanted to remove the pressure so I could mourn without the weight of planning her service.

I think she just didn't trust me to rent the right kind of confetti cannons.

I motioned toward the other side of the tent, where a woman in a floor-length brocade gown was rearranging the tables. "Once you clean up the beer stains, can you rein in your potluck friends before Burton finds them?"

Beverlee snorted. "She looks like a piece of secondhand furniture that you'd see sitting on the side of the highway."

"Could you get her to go outside and enjoy the festival for an hour or so?"

"How about I just instruct her to get down on her hands and knees and pretend to be an ottoman for an hour?" she suggested, a mischievous twinkle flashing through her eyes. "In fact, I could get the rest of the Methodist Ladies to participate, too. It would look like some sort of avant-garde art exhibit."

"More like the scratch and dent section at the Furniture Mart."

Just then, the bride and her entourage arrived. Ruby entered first, immediately followed by four of her college friends and her old roommate from New York City. Totty trailed behind them, and she was so focused on gawking at the decorations she stumbled into a potted plant on the way in and nearly dropped the foil-wrapped tray she was carrying.

"Happy wedding luncheon, Ruby!" I said, sweeping my hand around the room. "What do you think?"

Despite Burton's insistence that we move to square tables and Moe's desire to incorporate funeral linens, the location had turned out beautifully. White twinkle lights sparkled from the ceiling, greenery filled the corners, and serene arrangements of pink flowers anchored each table. Weathered window frames hung from chains along the outside edges of the tent's awning to separate the event space from the festival just beyond its edges.

"Beautiful, isn't it?" I asked, spinning back around to face Ruby.

But instead of the approval I expected, her expression was blank, and her eyes were red.

"Ruby?" I asked, looking toward her mother for guidance.

Totty returned my questioning gaze with a shrug, her mouth zipped into a stiff line.

I leaned in close and asked, "What happened? Did she get in an argument with Warren again?"

In the time I had been planning their wedding, those two had been in more fights than I could count. But just when I thought they'd finally break it off, she'd show up with a dazzling diamond necklace or he'd arrive on a fancy new motorcycle. Apparently, fighting was an aphrodisiac to them, although I never understood how someone would willingly sign up to spend their life with another human who made them miserable more often than happy.

I had been married to a jerk once upon a time, but even we liked each other on the days leading up to the wedding.

Ruby sniffled, and her mother dug down in her handbag to produce a tissue. "Warren hasn't checked in since he left to go fishing with his buddies," Totty whispered.

"Well, that's not unusual, is it?" I asked, plastering on my most your-future-husband-isn't-really-a-loser farce of a smile. "They probably don't have good reception out there on the open ocean."

I tried to be supportive, but doubted I was the only one

standing here who thought Ruby's fiancé probably had his face buried too far in someone else's cleavage to answer his cell phone.

"That's just it, though," Ruby said while she dabbed at her under-eye. "He was supposed to call me last night, and he didn't. So when I used the app on my phone that helps me track him, he wasn't anywhere near the water."

"Where was he?" I asked.

"Right here." She gestured toward the crowd of people moving around the festival right outside the party tent. "Warren was in downtown Flat Falls when he should have been on that boat."

I didn't mention the fact that many people would have considered her behavior stalking. Beverlee had installed that same app on my phone so I could find her quickly if she wound up on a bad date and needed a quick rescue. Instead, I patted Ruby's arm and prepared the "I'm sorry your fiancé is missing" speech that I'd had to give more often than I expected since becoming a wedding planner.

I took a deep breath and summoned my deep stores of patience. "I'm sure there's a perfectly good—"

"But the little red dot that shows me his location just… disappeared." Ruby's chin quivered as more tears threatened. "It's like he turned his phone off."

I wanted to remind her that turning his phone off wasn't the worst thing that could have happened to Warren Levi, but doubted it was good form to introduce thoughts of homicide or random STDs when your bride was feeling this anxious.

"Maybe he didn't go fishing after all," Totty suggested. She searched the room, her eyes widening as her gaze reached Beverlee and the Methodist brigade, who appeared to be doing calisthenics in the corner. "What if he decided to surprise you by showing up for your special day?"

Ruby's eyes lit up with hope as she followed her mother's gaze. "Do you think he would do that?"

Not a chance, I thought.

At the same time, my head involuntarily bobbed up and down and a breathy voice I hardly recognized replied, "That would be lovely."

When I ushered Ruby to the head table, she insisted on leaving a chair open in case Warren showed up. She even poured him a glass of sweet tea, which she said next to bourbon was his favorite.

As the guests filed in, though, that seat remained conspicuously empty, and the glass of tea began to sweat until it had left a new puddle on the already damp funeral tablecloths.

DESPITE THE GROOM'S ABSENCE, the luncheon seemed to be a success. Most of Flat Falls had shown up to offer Ruby their well-wishes, even if it meant they were dragging a chain of children whose hands were sticky from cotton candy or just came through to snag a chilled shrimp from the appetizer table.

I had to admit that Burton had done a fantastic job with the food, too. From the delicate melon cubes laced with sprigs of mint to the toasted bruschetta topped with cherries, prosciutto, and ricotta, every item coordinated with Lucy's chosen color palette, a mishmash of reds, pinks, and corals Beverlee had approvingly described as "fruit punch." And despite my worries that he would storm through the room knocking over the champagne fountain during a Godzilla-worthy tirade, Burton stayed in the food prep tent set up behind the main event area.

The gift table was piled high with boxes of all sizes

wrapped in shades of white with big, fluffy ribbons, and the mayor had made so many circuits around the room shaking hands and kissing babies I was sure he'd have sore hamstrings the next morning.

Even the bride seemed to be having fun. Ruby had given up staring at the entryway and had joined a group of her college friends for an awkward group conga when the DJ pushed aside a few square tables to create an impromptu dance floor. Eventually, they were joined by three of the Methodist Ladies, who hiked up their compression stockings and launched themselves into the fray.

I flashed an alarmed look at Beverlee, who seemed to be enjoying the show and wasn't at all concerned that a broken hip was imminent.

I rushed across the dance floor to her and said in an exaggerated whisper, "Beverlee, can you keep an eye on your friends, please? I love that they're having a good time, but I don't want to have to call an ambulance because Gert decided to pop and lock her way into a cardiac event."

We both swiveled toward the dancer in question just as she lifted her calf-length brocade skirt with both hands and gave a kick suitable for a Rockette's audition.

"Duck!" I screamed as her sensible shoe went flying across the dance floor, landing with a splash in the champagne fountain.

Gert's expression transformed from alarm to delight, and she whooped with laughter as she made her way over to us.

"I haven't had that much fun in years," she wheezed, her breath coming out in short pants. "And my bladder can't handle the excitement. I'm off for a quick trip to the little girls' room."

Tossing a breezy wave over her shoulder, she strolled

toward the back of the tent, stopping on the way to fish her navy pump out of the punch.

Now I'd have to get the catering staff to block off the fountain so other guests didn't have to taste Gert's socks.

"Should we tell her the bathroom's the other way?" I asked.

Beverlee shook her head. "No, she'll figure it out. It's time for dessert, anyway."

I checked my watch and agreed. "I'll head back to the kitchen and let Burton know."

I had just moved toward the serving area when a loud scream echoed through the tent. It went on for several seconds, and by the time the screeching ceased, the DJ had paused the music, and every single guest was glancing around for the source of the noise.

After motioning for the DJ to restart the music, I hurried across the dance floor in an awkward walk-run where I tried to look like I wasn't panicked.

But I was panicked.

Pushing through the back of the tent into the kitchen, I discovered Gert standing in the middle of the room hyperventilating while the waitstaff fanned her and shoved a glass of ice water into her shaking hands.

When she saw me, her eyes filled with tears, and she pointed to the freezer truck. "That's not the bathroom."

My gaze followed her finger, landing on the truck door that had been propped open with a stool.

With a gasp, I stepped forward, shocked to see Burton Levi stretched out in the middle of the freezer floor, eyes wide open and frozen in a scowl, his white apron stained red with blood.

14

Beverlee met me at the Grind and Go the next morning with a hazelnut latte and a sympathetic smile.

"I think I'm going to need two of these," I said, slurping from the plastic lid, not caring that the scalding liquid burned my throat as I swallowed. "Yesterday was terrible."

Cleaning up after parties has never been my favorite thing, but I hated it even more when the cleanup involved a visit from the coroner and the sacks of trash were accompanied by a body bag.

"At least it was out of sight. Most of the guests didn't even know anything had happened."

"Sure, it was out of sight until they rolled the body out through the middle of the dance floor."

"That was only because the coroner couldn't fit her truck behind the tent," Beverlee replied.

"And then they grilled the remaining guests before letting them leave," I said, willing the caffeine to stave off the tension headache building at the base of my skull.

"You gave them party favors, Glory," she said. "They were perfectly satisfied."

Somehow I doubted the small tins of Jordan almonds were enough to distract from the dead body that had crashed the party.

"What am I going to do?" I let my head fall to the table with a thunk. "First, we need to find the missing groom, and then I need to run by the office to grab the guest list so I can let people know the ceremony will be postponed while the groom's family grieves."

A shiny, patent leather purse hit the floor next to my feet. "That won't be necessary."

I whipped my head up to find Virginia Levi glaring at me, her son standing a few feet behind her, staring at his shoes.

I pushed the chair back with a scrape and jumped to my feet. "Virginia, I'm so sorry for your loss. I know you and Warren must be devastated."

She brushed past me and sat down at the table with Beverlee.

Blinking, I took in her calm demeanor. Maybe she was still in shock, but I imagined that if I had just lost my husband, I wouldn't be able to even dress myself, let alone drive across town to plan a party.

Then again, Burton Levi was a jerk, so maybe the rules of mourning didn't apply.

I tugged the chair out with my foot and sank into it, never taking my eyes off her face. Her makeup was pristine, her eyeliner perfectly intact, like she hadn't shed a tear over her husband's passing.

"Virginia, you've had quite a shock. Why don't you let Warren take you home to rest, and we'll contact your guests to postpone the ceremony?" I suggested.

She balled up a tissue from her pocket and dabbed underneath her still-dry eyes. "Warren, tell her."

He shuffled his feet one last time before raising his gaze to meet mine. "The wedding is still on."

I turned a questioning look toward Beverlee, who was watching the spectacle unfold with her cup of coffee as if it was a daytime soap opera. I sharpened my gaze, imploring her to speak up, but she just popped off the corner of her croissant and took a leisurely sip of her drink.

"I'm sorry," I said, pivoting back to Warren. "I must have misheard you. You're getting married in two days, and your father appears to have met an untimely and rather gruesome end. Yet you still want to—"

He nodded, his lips pressed into a grim line. "Yes. We'd like to continue with the arrangements."

I shifted my gaze between Warren and his mother. "And you're okay with this?"

She pulled her tablet out of her purse. "It's what Burton would have wanted, so we're moving forward as planned. I have all of his notes, and I spent the morning confirming the details with the vendors. I was afraid we'd have an issue without my husband here to handle the details, but frankly, most of them seemed just fine to move on without him."

I could imagine. From what I had seen of Burton's relationships with other people in the business, they would be relieved to get their hands on his obituary.

I searched Virginia's face for some sort of clarification, finally throwing my hands into the air. "I'm not sure I understand. First, your son was missing. Then your husband… It's a lot to take in."

"I wasn't missing." Warren hooked a thumb loosely through his belt loop. "I was on the boat. Just like I told you I was going to be."

"Then why was your phone at the festival?" I rubbed my temple with the back side of a spoon.

He narrowed his eyes as he considered me, finally lifting his shoulder in a half-hearted shrug. "I lost it."

Beverlee pointed to the bulge in his back pocket. "Found it again, too, did you?"

He slipped the phone out of his pocket and studied it like he wasn't sure how it had gotten there. "Yes. Somebody turned it into the lost and found near the front of Town Hall."

Virginia patted her son's arm. "That's my boy. Always losing things. Marrying Ruby will be the best thing that has happened to him. She'll help him keep his head on straight."

Warren's eyes were unfocused, and from his rumpled clothes to the sagging of his shoulders, I could tell that the last few days had hit him harder than he was letting on. Although he and Burton hadn't seemed close during our recent meetings, it was still an earthshattering blow to lose your father.

I should know.

"And have you confirmed that Ruby's still on board with the ceremony plans?" I asked.

The tinkling of bells above the door to the coffee shop signaled a new arrival, and we all swiveled to see Ruby walk in, fresh and lovely in a yellow gingham dress, her hair flowing loosely around her shoulders.

She stood on her tiptoes and kissed Warren on the cheek, then slid her hand into his. "What did I miss?"

"We were just talking about how to move forward with your wedding plans, given the unfortunate circumstances," I answered. "And the Levis have been so brave. Both Virginia and Warren said they want to proceed with the ceremony."

Ruby exhaled dramatically and turned to her future

husband and his mother. "I know. It's so generous of them to put aside their grief to allow us to continue."

The snort that escaped didn't play well with the cup I had just pressed to my mouth, so I inadvertently sent a shower of coffee across the table. I wiped it off with my sleeve and tried to clear my throat. "So generous," I replied, pretending Virginia Levi's crisp linen blouse wasn't sporting a handful of tiny new stains. It was also weird and bordering on inappropriate to move forward so soon after the tragedy. Burton Levi was face-up in a drawer at the county morgue, not on a last-minute business trip to Cincinnati.

But Virginia nodded in agreement, her chin trembling as the tears finally began to fall. She sniffled into a tissue. "He put so much time into the reception menu, and I know it would break his heart to have all that food go to waste just because he had…"

"Expired?" Beverlee supplied gently.

"Surely he'd understand your need to grieve," I said. "And as newlyweds, you deserve to start your lives together on a day not overshadowed by such a sad occurrence."

"No, it's fine," Ruby said, leaning her head on Warren's shoulder. "Burton would have wanted it this way."

Virginia fiddled with her tissue before finally turning a watery smile to her son and future daughter-in-law. "And besides, these two have a plane to catch on Monday morning. Honeymoons wait for nobody."

Warren kissed the top of Ruby's head. "I'm really looking forward to a week on the beach. It's been so long since I've had a vacation."

I didn't mention that his whole life was one long vacation, interspersed with a day here and there hanging out at the restaurant with his father and adding in surfing or golf on the weekend.

"You're still going to Saint Croix next week?" I asked Ruby.

"Of course," Virginia interjected. "They get a week to enjoy their new life together, and then Warren needs to come back to take over the restaurant and all of Burton's contracts and special projects."

LATER THAT EVENING, I was sitting on my living room floor surrounded by takeout containers while Beverlee, Scoots, and Josie consoled me over Burton's death. Not because he had died, because goodness knows there hadn't been many people out there who deserved to meet their maker more than that Neanderthal, but because his death left me without another suspect.

"We were so close to proving that Burton had killed Rocky," I said, pausing to disrupt my pout with a large slice of naan bread. I ripped off a hunk and swiped it through the butter chicken sauce on my paper plate. "And now he's dead. How am I supposed to clear my father's name if Burton is dead?"

"Did you get a good look at the body?" Scoots asked, her face bright. "Did he look like somebody who had been murdered?"

"And what, exactly, does it look like to be murdered?" Beverlee bounced her straw around in her tea. "Maybe he slipped on an errant banana peel or his own ego and then hit his head on the counter."

Josie put down her fork and pulled her laptop toward her. "I saw an article about him on the news today. I wasn't paying a lot of attention because he had it coming to him. But I think they have officially classified it as a murder."

My stomach rolled as I remembered the blood stains on

Burton's apron. "You think? He was lying on the floor in a pool of his blood. That generally doesn't happen by accident."

"Look who's an expert on murder now," Beverlee responded.

And she was right. I had seen far more bodies than I wanted to in the last year. Who knew weddings could be so deadly?

Just as I was about to forego the fork and drop my face directly to the plate in front of me, a brief knock sounded at my door.

"Who could that be?" Beverlee asked, hopping up from the sofa and crossing to the door.

Chief Goodnight stood just outside, his face obscured by the shadow cast from the porch light and his hands stuffed into his uniform pockets. When he saw Beverlee, he straightened his shoulders and flipped off his hat.

"Hello, Hollis." Beverlee patted her hair. "We're just having some supper. Would you care to join us?"

He cast a longing look at the feast spread out in front of us. Scoots had hit more than one takeout joint on her way over because she wasn't sure what appetizer was the most appropriate for mourning a death when you didn't actually care about the deceased.

"Sorry, I can't stay," he said. "But I thought I'd come by and give you ladies an update on the investigation."

"On Burton?" I asked. "Do you know what happened?"

Hollis shook his head. "Can't really talk about Mr. Levi's case, but we're working with Big River police on a joint investigation."

"If you let Wayne Daly handle anything having to do with your investigation, you're just asking for trouble," Beverlee said. "He's not nearly as qualified as you are."

The skin underneath Hollis's scruff reddened, but he

cleared his throat and continued. "This isn't about yesterday's incident," he said, his gaze catching mine. "I came by to update you on the murder of Rocky Boyd."

The chicken turned to rocks in my stomach. "What have you found?"

"We referred your uncle's remains to a forensic anthropologist in Raleigh. As a favor to me, she has already sent over her preliminary report."

"And?" I searched his face for information, but the frown that stretched his lips into a grim line had me wanting to stick my fingers into my ears to keep from hearing his news.

"There were skull fractures consistent with blows to the head."

"English, please," Beverlee instructed.

Scoots leaned forward, her forearms resting on her knees. "It means Rocky died from getting hit upside the head. Which also means, in lawyer-speak, that the investigators will be classifying his death as a homicide."

I jerked myself to my feet. "Is that true?"

Hollis gave a solemn nod. "I'm afraid so."

"But it was a long time ago," I said. "How can they tell?"

"His body was well-protected in its little pig-topped tomb. "They're even running DNA analysis on the leather jacket, although they're not hopeful that blood stains would have survived this long."

I gripped the back of the sofa for stability. "What does all this mean?"

"That's what I came to tell you. We have a handful of witnesses who were downtown at the festival that night and claim to have seen your father hit Rocky just before he disappeared."

"So? How many times do I have to repeat this?" I replied. "They were brothers. Brothers fight."

"The mayor's office went back through old purchase orders and provided us a schedule for the installation of the pig sculpture." Hollis took a deep breath. "It was installed the morning after your parents were killed."

"What are you saying, Hollis?" Beverlee asked.

"My investigators have pieced together the timeline, and they feel confident that Daniel Boyd killed his brother just before the accident that took his life."

"No!" Indignation flashed hot in my chest. "You knew my father. You *know* he wouldn't have done this."

He dropped his gaze to the ground for a moment before reaching out to put a hand on my shoulder. "I wanted to let you know in person. We should be getting the final report from Raleigh in a few days, and then we'll close the case."

"You can't close it," I screeched. "My father didn't kill anyone!"

"Glory, I wish I had better news, but you know as well as I do that we just don't have the resources to pursue this any further. Cold cases like this don't get a lot of our attention as it is, but even less when the primary suspect isn't around to receive justice. I'm sorry."

With a sympathetic tip of his hat, Hollis left us alone. As soon as the soft click of the door shutting echoed through the room, Josie turned to me. "What now?"

"You just heard Chief Goodnight. I have two days to figure out who killed Rocky Boyd before they close the case, and my father is permanently labeled as a murderer. And then I have to run a wedding that will erase a hundred years of rivalry." I deposited my still-full dinner plate on the counter as a wave of terror rolled through me. "No big deal."

15

Bang. *Bang. Bang.*

The knocking interrupted an excellent dream I was having about a couple of wayward soldiers and a bag of melted chocolate chips.

Josie and I had stayed up late the night before, our eyes glued to her laptop screen as we searched for a clue that would help us figure out who had killed my uncle. But as the clock neared midnight, our eyes glazed over, and we decided to watch a Civil War-era romance while eating cookie dough straight out of the tube.

I swept my gaze around the room for Josie, who had apparently gone back to her apartment at some point in the wee hours of the morning, leaving me covered in a blanket with my face pressed into the sofa cushions.

"Glory," Beverlee called from outside the door. "Open up. We have important things to do."

When I didn't budge, she let herself in.

I pushed myself up on my arms and peered over the back of the sofa with one eye still closed. "No," I replied, sagging back down underneath the blanket. "I have too much work today to go off on one of your tangents."

The curtains scraped across the metal rod as she opened them, blasting the room with morning light.

I popped up again, sweeping the back of my hand across my eyes. "What time is it? I've got to get to the office. I have a meeting with Ruby and Totty this morning at eight o'clock."

"It's nine."

"What?" I shrieked, stumbling across the floor, trying to put my pants on while brushing my hair. "I can't believe I did this. I thought I set an alarm."

My stomach plummeted as I grabbed my phone from the coffee table and saw its black screen. "My phone is dead."

I scrambled around the living room, finally peeling the cookie dough wrapper from the top of my shoe. Acid burned in my chest, a testament to what a bucket of sugar will do to a thirty-something digestive system. "I need—"

"Coffee?" Beverlee suggested, thrusting her arm out to offer a steaming paper cup with the Grind and Go logo on it.

I lurched toward the lifeline. "Bless you. And can I borrow your phone? I need to call and apologize to Ruby."

"No need. I met them at the office this morning. Everything is on track for the wedding tomorrow."

"How did you—?"

"I was already there getting things ready. When you didn't show up or answer your phone, I got worried," she said, deftly folding the blanket I had tossed on the floor. She rested it on the back of the sofa. "I called Josie, and she told me you were up late trying to help your daddy. I was disappointed you weren't off with an exotic stranger you met at a beach bar, but you have been very stressed these days, and you're not exactly putting off 'come and get me, boys' vibes."

I took a long sip of coffee before responding. "First of all, thank you for saving the day. I owe you one of Shirley's famous chocolate cakes."

Shirley normally served fresh scones and muffins behind the counter at the Grind and Go, but if you slipped her a twenty and begged, she'd mix up a mocha masterpiece with three layers of chocolate cake and a heaping pile of decadent ganache. I had been using Shirley's cakes to weasel my way out of trouble since I was a teenager, and it was well worth the hundreds of dollars Shirley had pocketed to stay on Beverlee's good side.

"And second," I added, shooting her a scowl, "I'm knee-deep in planning a wedding between two people who don't even like each other half the time, my caterer-slash-father-of-the-groom was just found belly-up next to a tray of strawberry tarts, there's a rumor that a sleazeball is my daddy, and my actual father has been blamed for a murder he didn't commit. What makes you think I'd have time for an exotic stranger?"

"Wishful thinking? Besides, all this talk about Daniel and Lucy has reminded me that I promised to look after you. That includes making sure you live happily ever after."

"Thank you for everything you've done for me. They would have been proud," I said, wrapping my arms around her in a tight squeeze. When her stomach nipped at me, I jumped back.

"What is that?" I yelped. "You always swore you'd pay for a chest that bit back, but I didn't think Venus fly boobs were actually a thing."

She pulled aside her loose chambray shirt just as Matilda popped her head out from the baby carrier strapped across her torso.

"You're baby-wearing your chicken?" I demanded.

"Of course." She tucked Matilda's head back between the folds of fabric. "It keeps her comfortable and then she doesn't go around stealing food from strangers."

Matilda's favorite fare was cookies, and even though Beverlee regularly baked her special treats laden with veggie scraps and mealworms, she had been known to steal a snickerdoodle or two while she was out and about.

"Why is your chicken here?" I asked, my fingers already heading to the knot in my shoulders that accompanied any journey with Beverlee and her chicken.

"We're going to Big River to introduce Matilda to her future husband," she replied, flashing me a sharp glare. "Somebody in this family is going to get married, and if it's not you, it's got to be her."

I ignored her jab and instead glanced over her shoulder. "We?"

Beverlee nodded. "Scoots is already down in your car reprogramming the radio stations to eighties hair bands."

"What's wrong with your car?"

"Nothing. But we figured Matilda would make a better first impression if she arrived in a flashy sports car. We wouldn't want Phil to think that she's a wallflower."

I doubted Phil Donahue would have those thoughts about the hen riding in the rainbow sling with the words "cluck this" embroidered in hot pink across the front.

"And besides," Beverlee added with a knowing look. "It will give you the perfect opportunity to do a bit of snooping around Big River. I heard they're having a craft show downtown, and it will be a great place to get some answers about your family."

～

Scoots had insisted on driving, which meant she had cranked the radio all the way up and rolled the windows all the way down. So not only was my stomach roiling from her inability to take corners at a normal speed, but my hair was sticking out so far I was sure the seagulls flitting above thought I was an over-puffed sand dune.

She dropped me off at the edge of the craft fair and instructed me not to return until I had answers. I wasn't sure how to solve a decades-old crime in three aisles of shell crafts and homemade cherry jam, but I was relieved to have a break from the high-volume electric guitars that still echoed through my brain from the car ride over.

I ran my fingers along a sheet of handmade paper at the first stall and wondered if it would be impolite to rip off a piece to stuff into my ears to stop the ringing.

The woman behind the table nodded approvingly at my choice. "It's one of my favorites. I incorporated some of the hair my little Fritz left on my velvet loveseat." She stroked a tiny white dog leashed to a table leg while I tried not to gag.

"That's one way to recycle." I fought the urge to wipe my fingers on my jeans as I leaned in to inspect the fibers. Sure enough, fine white hairs were mixed into the gray paper. Upon further inspection, I discovered they also wound their way through the weave of her sleeveless sweater, and I couldn't decide if I should walk away or pet her.

"I haven't seen you around here before," she said, offering me a friendly smile. "Are you new in town?"

"No, I'm just visiting this morning. I came to offer my condolences to the Levi family."

"Isn't it the most awful thing? Poor Virginia." She pressed her palm to her chest. "I hope now that Burton is out of the way, she'll be able to live in peace."

I nodded in agreement, whispering, "I take it you weren't a fan."

She sized me up with narrowed eyes before pointing to the stack of paper. "I could just ramble on and on. Shall I roll the paper for you while we talk?" she asked with far too innocent a smile for a geriatric extortionist.

"Of course," I agreed, reaching into my pocket for my wallet. I knew when I was getting played, and I just hoped she had information that was worth the price of carrying around dog fur for the rest of the morning.

She carefully packaged up my purchase and tied the roll with a strip of raffia, and then handed it across the table with a flourish. "I'd never talk ill of the dead, but since you're a customer, I'll make an exception. Burton Levi was a stain on the underpants of humanity."

A gross description, but I didn't disagree.

"The only time we ever really saw Virginia was at the library," the woman continued. "We've been asking her to join our quilting circle for years, but she always said she needed to be there for Burton and the baby."

"The baby?" I asked.

She nodded. "Yes, Warren."

Warren Levi might act like a baby most of the time, but he was over thirty years old.

"And I'm not one to stick my nose into other people's business," she said, doing exactly that, "but I always thought that there was something off with Burton. All those business deals. Did you ever wonder why nobody else ever won a contract when they went up against him?"

She didn't even wait for a response. Instead, she plucked another piece of paper up and rolled it into a tube, which she waved around in the air to emphasize her points. "He was some sort of business shark, buying all that land and leaving the mom-and-pop shops out of work in his wake."

I ducked as she came a little too close to swatting me in the eye. "What kind of land?" I asked, interest prickling along the back of my neck.

She swept her hand out wide in front of her, this time catching my collar. "He owns at least half the properties along the waterfront. Bullied his way into them, no doubt. And just imagine what it must have been like to be married to the man."

I didn't have to work too hard to imagine that one. My almost-ex-husband, Cobb Mulvaney, was bossy and demanding, too—only instead of emptying other people's bank accounts, he emptied mine.

After I declined the artist's offer to sell me a journal made from her dryer lint, she moved on to help another customer, and I was left to wonder how Virginia had lived for so many decades under the thumb of her oppressive husband. The stress of Warren's wedding might have finally pushed her over the edge.

~

MY UBER PULLED up in front of my grandmother's house just in time for me to see her newspaper curtains pop open.

I gave her a finger wave as I hopped out of the car and walked toward Bud's backyard. Bud and Scoots sat at a patio table with a large green umbrella, while Beverlee rested cross-legged on the grass, petting the top of Matilda's head.

My aunt glanced up at me, her face drawn.

"What's wrong?" I asked.

Beverlee sniffed. "Phil Donahue isn't interested in us."

I looked to Scoots for clarification. She pointed across the yard, where the rooster was pecking at a patch of grass that was decidedly not near his future chicken bride.

A chuckle bubbled out from the center of my chest, and I bit my bottom lip. Beverlee's expression was as sad as the time her doctor told her she needed to cut down on cheddar cheese because her cholesterol was going up.

I flopped onto the grass next to her and offered my most supportive smile. "Some chickens just take a little while to warm up. They're like men in that way. How many guys do you know that would cozy up to a woman he'd just met when she comes barreling in wanting to tie him down?"

Beverlee scoffed. "My Louis said he wanted to marry me from the moment he saw me."

Beverlee's first husband had set the standard by which she'd evaluate men for the rest of her life. And since nobody had ever lived up to him, she had been on the prowl for husband number four ever since he had passed away choking on a chicken bone nearly two decades ago.

She fluttered her eyelashes at Bud, but he wasn't paying attention. Instead, he was focused on Scoots, who kept flashing him an annoyed glare whenever they'd make eye contact.

I turned back toward Beverlee. "Maybe Matilda just needs to spend the rest of her days being a bachelorette," I suggested gently.

She studied me. "Just because she's entered her change of life, it doesn't mean she's not entitled to find love."

"Her what?" I asked, certain we weren't actually talking about poultry hormones.

"Chicken menopause." Beverlee leaned toward me and lowered her voice to explain. "She stopped laying eggs. But that doesn't mean she doesn't still have a lot to offer the world."

"No, of course not." I backpedaled at Beverlee's indignant huff. Although she had shifted her gaze back toward

Matilda, I had a sneaking suspicion we weren't just talking about her favorite hen. "Every lady deserves romance, no matter her age."

Or species, apparently.

Satisfied that I understood her predicament, Beverlee pushed herself off the ground, releasing Matilda to wander through the grass. She brushed off her pants with her fingertips.

"How did it go over at the festival?" she asked.

"I got a lovely piece of handmade paper made from dog hair," I replied. "It's going to be your Christmas present."

"That's very kind of you. What else?"

"I discovered that Burton has been buying up pieces of property adjacent to his restaurant. It sounds like he's been doing it by brute force, and a lot of the residents of Big River aren't happy about it."

"Well, that's a start." Her mouth fell open as she watched both Matilda and Phil Donahue trot across the lawn toward Scoots from opposite directions.

Scoots swiveled her body to move her feet away from the chicken onslaught. "Shoo," she said, brushing them away. "I don't like you."

When they continued pecking around beneath her, Bud jumped to his feet. He grabbed Phil, wrapping his large hands securely around the chicken's wings as his lined face turned an endearing shade of pink. "Sorry about that," he mumbled. As soon as he sat back down with Phil in his lap, Matilda started clucking at his feet.

"What do you want, Matilda?" Bud asked.

She batted her head against his ankle.

"I think she wants you to pick her up," Beverlee said.

"This isn't a petting zoo," he replied with a gruff voice, grasping Matilda underneath her chest and dragging her to his lap.

She pranced up and down his thighs before settling down next to Phil.

"Oh!" Beverlee clapped her hands excitedly and rushed toward the table. But as soon as she got close enough, Matilda hopped down and trotted over to Scoots again.

Beverlee's forehead creased, and the entire scene started all over, with Matilda bouncing back and forth between Bud and Scoots.

"I think your chicken is playing matchmaker," I whispered to Beverlee while Matilda distracted the other two with flapping wings and clucks of delight.

Beverlee considered them with a furrowed brow. "Bud and… Scoots?" she asked, her brows flattening even more as if the whole idea didn't compute.

I patted her arm in consolation. "That's okay, Beverlee. We have a murder to solve. We don't need to be distracted by men who don't return our affections."

"I don't understand," she said. "Every time he gets near me, he gets flustered and goes mute. That normally happens when a man is working up his nerve to ask me to have crab legs at the all-you-can-eat seafood buffet, not when he's thinking about hitting on my best friend."

That part was true, at least. I'd seen more than a few men fumble over themselves in Beverlee's presence.

I was pondering the growing flush on Scoot's cheeks when a loud, crackling voice sounded from behind me.

"Have you found out who killed my son yet?"

I whipped around to see my grandmother, dressed in a fawn-colored housecoat and her usual slippers, shuffling toward us.

Beverlee, who always had her company manners tucked away in her back pocket, reacted first. "Hello, Ada. You're looking lovely today."

Ada didn't even acknowledge her. Instead, her gaze was laser-focused on me. "Well?" she asked.

"I'm working on it," I admitted. "Things have gotten a bit complicated."

"Complicated how?" she asked. "I'm not asking you to solve world hunger. I just want to know what happened to my Rocky. What could be more important than that?"

I swallowed the annoyed curse dancing at the edge of my tongue. "I'm sure you know we're in the middle of the Founder's Day Festival, and that this year it will feature a wedding."

"And?" she prompted.

"And I'm in charge of planning the wedding," I replied, hoping my grandmother might take an interest in something I was doing for once.

She brushed that idea away. "That whole family is no good. They don't deserve a happily ever after."

"But I thought Burton was Rocky's best friend," I said. "Surely you'd have some sympathy for his wife and son now that he met an untimely end."

"There always was something strange about that boy, even when he was in high school. And if Burton ever really was Rocky's friend, why did he let him disappear for all those years?" Ada shook her head. "I always said that a kid that comes from trash wouldn't amount to anything, anyway."

I didn't have an answer, so I rose from the grass and stared at Matilda, who was now pecking at the laces of Scoots's sneaker. If that was true, it didn't bode well for my father's chances. But he had escaped from Big River and built a family and a respectable career. The first sting of tears formed at the corners of my eyes as I marveled at all he had gone through to establish his new life, and the thought of somebody running his reputation back through the dirt he had come from was almost too much for me to bear.

Beverlee watched me start to unravel, and as she had been doing since I was a six-year-old who used to hide under her kitchen sink, she stepped in to protect me.

She sprang in front of me with her finger wagging in Ada's face, her voice loud and commanding and without even an ounce of its normal buoyancy. "What about you? What have you done to find your son's killer?"

Ada took in a deep breath. "I figured I wouldn't leave it to Little Miss Incompetent over there. I'm doing a little investigating of my own."

"What does that mean?" I demanded, my irritation rising more quickly than my ability to keep my mouth closed.

"It means that since you can't seem to do your job, I'm going to have to do it for you." She brushed a stiff hand over her housedress. "We're going out on the town to find out who killed my boy."

"We?" Scoots and I asked at the same time.

Ada scowled, and for a moment she stopped looking like a lonely old woman and started to resemble a serial killer who would enjoy eating my kidneys topped with a bit of marmalade for breakfast.

Beverlee mouthed, "No," and shook her head so frantically one of her earrings flew off and landed on Bud's table.

But Ada Boyd must have been the genetic origin of the stubborn streak that flowed so freely down through my father to me. It didn't take long before I found myself crammed in between her and Beverlee in the back seat of Bud's SUV. Since he had the only car that could fit all of us, we volunteered him as our official chauffeur for the afternoon.

We left Matilda and Phil Donahue in Bud's garden for

what Beverlee called a marriage dry run. In my mind, this meant that by the time we returned, Phil would be lounging under the shade of a honeysuckle vine while Matilda ran around gathering bugs for him.

"I call shotgun," Scoots said as Ada swapped her house shoes for a pair of yellow gardening clogs she found in a pile of mulch next to her front porch.

"I don't want to sit with her," I whispered, practically pushing Scoots down to claim the front seat before she did.

But Scoots won out by hip-checking me, which because she was so much shorter, felt almost like I had taken a baton to the thigh. "She's your granny, toots. This is all on you."

16

———

"What's the plan?" Bud asked as he pulled to a stop in front of Lavish. "Are we just going to prowl around out here and ask if anybody knows who killed Rocky?"

I had been sandwiched between my grandmother and Beverlee for the last twenty minutes, and I would have done any amount of prowling he suggested just to get out of the car. Even though Ada hadn't talked much, she spent most of the ride alternating between glaring at Bud in the mirror and trying to embed her elbow in my rib cage to gain more room on the bench seat.

"It's almost lunchtime," Beverlee said, squeezing my knee gently. "Everybody knows the best place to get answers is from the inside."

I wasn't sure if it was because she knew how I was feeling or if she had just gotten a hankering for fried flounder, but it didn't matter. I bobbed my head up and down and practically threw myself after her onto the sidewalk when she opened the car door.

"Can we go in there like this?" Beverlee asked,

motioning to her own capri pants and sandals while her eyes skated over Ada's house dress.

Ada had tucked a loose gray sweater around her shoulders as we left her house, but from the looks of her fingertips poking out through the front pockets, it might have been a retreat for small rodents before she turned it into outerwear. Bud assured us we would be fine, and he went ahead into the restaurant to reserve a table.

When we followed him a few minutes later, we were greeted warmly, and nobody pointed out that more than one member of our party was wearing gardening attire. I would have pegged him as a miracle worker, except I saw him slip the hostess a twenty from his wallet as she ushered us toward a table bordering the water.

I raised a brow in challenge, but he smiled and held the chair out for Scoots. Scoots didn't seem to appreciate the effort and moved to another chair, kicking it out with the toe of her tennis shoe and plopping onto it with a huff.

After the server asked for our drink order, Ada leaned toward him and asked, "What do you know about murder?"

He jumped back as if he feared we were going to slice him into bits right there on the freshly pressed white tablecloth. When we convinced him that all we actually wanted was a pitcher of ice water with lemons, he shuffled away, refusing to turn his back on us.

I glared at my grandmother, who was digging through the bread basket. "Perhaps we need to have a discussion about subtlety. Nobody's going to give up information when they're worried you're going to decapitate them in the middle of a shift."

"And perhaps that's the reason you haven't figured out who killed Rocky. You're too weak, and nobody takes you seriously." With that, she pushed back from her seat and rose. "I'm going to see what I can find out."

I started to go after her—more to keep her from ruining what little social currency we had established on our way in than out of concern—but Beverlee restrained me. "Just let her go. What kind of trouble could she get into?"

That question was answered less than ten minutes later when the wail of the fire alarm disrupted our appetizer course. I looked mournfully at the freshly delivered plate of steamed oysters as we gathered our things.

"This way, please," the server instructed, herding the crowd toward the exit. Bud had Scoots's satchel over one arm, while his other hand rested on the small of her back.

Beverlee pointed at it and wiggled her eyebrows.

I debated leaving Ada to deal with whatever chaos she had unleashed, but then the guilt settled in. I tapped the server on the shoulder and gestured toward the restroom down the hall. "I'm sorry, but my grandmother went to the ladies' room, and she's hard of hearing. She might not be able to hear the sirens."

He glanced up at the flashing red light on the exit sign. "You need to exit immediately, ma'am."

That's when Beverlee elbowed past me and waggled her finger in his face. "You're going to let an old woman die alone in a public bathroom? Shame on you. What would your mama say?"

Only Beverlee could get away with invoking somebody's mother as a form of blackmail, but it seemed to work. He dropped his head and told us to hurry. "If they find out I let you back in there, I'll get fired."

Beverlee gave him a grateful smile, grabbed my wrist, and yanked me down the hall.

We entered the bathroom, and Beverlee's expression turned from annoyance to admiration. "Look," she said, gaping at the counter. "They have three different hand lotions for you to choose from. That's impressive."

I kicked open each stall before meeting her eyes in the mirror. "Ada's not in here."

"Where could she be?" Beverlee asked, massaging a lilac-scented cream onto her elbows.

I nudged her back toward the hallway and started toward a stairway I had noticed a moment before. "Up there."

The screeching of the alarm clanged inside my head as I dragged Beverlee up the stairs.

"Ada had better have a good explanation for this," Beverlee shouted, "because that was a delicious-looking plate of shrimp in front of me, and now I'll have to get my bag dry-cleaned." She fished a shrimp out of her tote and popped it into her mouth.

Just then, a door cracked open at the top of the stairs. I was preparing my best "I'm lost" face when Ada stuck her head out into the hall.

"What took you so long?" she snapped. "You missed my signal."

"Your signal was pulling the fire alarm?" I asked. "Couldn't you have tried something that wouldn't summon law enforcement?"

She ignored me. "Look what I found," she said, showing us a trash can next to the credenza.

"Garbage?" I asked. "You made me give up oysters Rockefeller because you found a bag of garbage in somebody's office?"

She rolled her eyes. "Look closer."

I picked up the slip of paper at the top of the pile. "Looks like an invoice," I said, gesturing around the room. "Burton ran a restaurant. There are probably thousands of invoices in here."

Ada pointed to the bag with more urgency. "I pulled the fire alarm because Burton's wife was in here shredding documents as fast as she could. I hid in the office next door until I saw her leave."

"So? She's got a business to run now."

"Don't be obtuse," she said. "The only reason Virginia is shredding all of this paperwork the day after her husband died is because she has something to hide."

Her logic was surprisingly sound, but that didn't make me any more eager to rummage through somebody's trash. I nudged the can with the tip of my shoe and grimaced as an apple core tumbled to the floor.

Suddenly, the fire alarm stopped ringing, and I glanced out the window to see three police cars and two fire engines idling outside.

"We've got to go," Beverlee warned.

So I did the only thing a rational woman like me could do. I stuffed the garbage bag under my shirt and waddled out of the office with Beverlee and Ada trailing me.

I HAD JUST SNAPPED rubber gloves on my hands when a loud scratch, followed by a thud, sounded outside my apartment door. I jumped up and stuck my face to the peephole, surprised to see Ian on the other side, waving a takeout bag in the air.

When I flung the door open, Rusty tumbled inside, barked, and rolled over in front of me.

"Sorry, I should have warned you," Ian said. "My dog was holding up your door from the outside."

I scratched Rusty's exposed belly, his fur soft under my fingers. "Who's a good boy?"

Ian shook the takeout bag. "Me," he answered with a flirty grin.

I yanked the bag from his outstretched hand and rustled

it open to get a whiff. "You brought me wings?" I asked, swooning a bit more than I should over a T-shirt clad man bearing a stinky dog and a pile of meat.

"And a batch of hushpuppies with honey butter."

I brought the bag in close and inhaled again, wondering if the food was the only thing responsible for the warmth spreading through my chest.

Ian's gaze zeroed in on my gloved fingers. "Are you doing some sort of medical exam in here?"

I motioned to the table, where I had spread out a handful of paperwork from the trash can at Lavish. "I'm investigating."

He raised a brow. "Do I even want to know?"

"It involved Beverlee and a gaggle of firefighters," I explained. "So probably not."

The gloves snapped again when I pulled them off to grab a set of plates from the kitchen. As I divided the food, I filled him in on the morning's activities.

"You're going through somebody's garbage," he said. "But you don't know who?"

I settled back onto the sofa next to him and shoved a drumette into my mouth to avoid answering.

"And you're looking for something, but you don't know what."

I dabbed a bit of ranch dressing from my lips with a napkin before nodding. "Pretty much."

"Okay." He appraised the garbage bag, which was still almost full on the floor next to me. "I'm in."

"Seriously?" I asked.

"Sure. It's not every day you get to go through a rival's trash. Maybe I'll find the recipe for Burton's secret sauce somewhere in there."

Intrigued, I leaned forward, knocking my napkin to the floor in front of me. "He's got a secret sauce?"

"Nah." He smirked, kicking a foot up on his opposite knee and settling back onto the sofa. "He thought it was a secret, but we all knew it was just off-the-shelf tartar sauce with a squirt of ketchup."

"Speaking of secrets, I was down on the waterfront in Big River this morning, and someone told me Burton had been buying up properties down there. Do you know what that's all about?"

He tossed Rusty a hush puppy from his plate, his expression grim. "I've been wondering the same thing. Several of the best restaurants in Big River have gone out of business. They were good people, Glory. It doesn't make sense."

Ian talked about the other restaurant owners in the area as if they were friends, not rivals—except Burton Levi. Everybody talked about him like he was the stuff they scraped out of the bottom of the fryer at the end of a long shift.

We settled into companionable silence as we shuffled through the rest of the bag's contents. Now and then, Ian grumbled about Burton getting a great price for romaine lettuce or gloated that Trolls had sold more shellfish in September.

"Right now, I'm wishing Burton wasn't so old-school and that we were paging through files on a laptop instead of digging through actual trash." I rolled my shoulders and held up a folded piece of paper. "But you'll be happy to know that the dermatologist says the mole she removed from Burton's shoulder was benign."

Ian shifted in his seat. "I should probably feel uncomfortable digging through a dead man's garbage can, but it's actually sort of interesting. You can find out a lot about a person from the things he throws away." As proof, he fished a shiny mailer out of the bag and held it up for my inspection. I recognized the line drawing of the bridge that was the centerpiece of the Trolls logo. "This is a perfectly good coupon."

"I guess he wasn't impressed by your offer for a free appetizer," I said, wiggling my fingers so he'd hand it over. "But I am."

He dropped the coupon in the trash pile. "You don't need a coupon. All you need to do is come in. Half of my staff has a crush on you as it is."

I wanted to ask him which half he fell into, but I chickened out and shifted my attention to a folder filled with stacks of graphs and spreadsheets. My hand covered a gasp as I realized what they were.

"What is it?" Ian asked.

I showed him the first printout, a neatly organized memo from a local business accounting firm. "It looks like a business valuation."

He slipped the folder from my fingers and shuffled through the stack, his eyebrows furrowing as he read. "There are dozens of them here. All local restaurants. He's got their tax information and an estimate of what they owe on their properties." Then he muttered a curse, and his hands got still.

"Ian?"

He slipped a page out of the stack. "He's got a valuation of Trolls. It looks like my restaurant was on his radar."

"Did he ever approach you?"

Ian shook his head, his fist clenched around the paper. "No. He knew better than that. I'm not looking to sell, but even if I were, I'd rather burn the place to the ground than sell it to Burton Levi."

I rested my hand on his knee and peered over his shoulder to get a better look at the document. "Wow, whoever put this together was very thorough. No wonder he could outbid his competition. He knew where everybody's weak spots were."

Ian dropped the folder back on the coffee table, his lips still drawn into a thin line. "But why?"

He rose and paced in front of the sofa. But when the drawstring of the garbage bag got caught up beneath his shoe, he stumbled, causing Rusty to bolt to his feet with an alarmed howl.

Ian righted himself quickly, but not before Rusty took off around the room, frantically barking at the invisible intruder.

The piles we had so carefully assembled went flying as he scrambled, and I grabbed my glass of water before his frenetic tail knocked it to the ground.

"Rusty, down," Ian ordered, and the dog dropped to the carpet, his body still twitching with anticipation. Ian grimaced as he surveyed the damage. "Sorry about that."

"I'm used to it," I replied, running my fingers over Rusty's soft, floppy ears. Grievous offense forgotten, he rolled over to present his belly, exposing a colorful rectangle of paper on the carpet beneath him.

I inspected the postcard with a sigh. It showed a beautiful waterfall surrounded by tropical flowers and inscribed with the words *Wish you were here.*

I waved it in the air. "Look at this sunrise. I need a vacation."

But as I was fantasizing about a few days of relaxing on the beach with a fruity cocktail, I noticed the back of the card. In scratchy handwriting, so small it was hardly legible, it read:

Sorry to leave town without saying goodbye. The chicks here are hot. - R

. . .

"It's a postcard from Rocky!" I exclaimed, bringing it up to my nose to make out the postmark. "And it's dated from the same year my parents died."

"Can you make out the month?" he asked.

I squinted and passed it in front of the lamp for extra light. "It's smudged. But this is something—it shows that Rocky might not have died the same night as his brother, and we're one step closer to proving my father's innocence."

~

Hollis brought his reading glasses to the tip of his nose, finally sliding them off and resting them on the edge of his desk beside the postcard.

"Do I want to know where you got this?" he asked, his eyes constricting as he studied me.

"Probably not," I answered, shooting a glance at Ian, who had accompanied me to the station on his way to work.

Hollis flipped the card over in his fingers and tapped it on the desk before leaning back. His chair gave a loud creak of protest, but Hollis didn't seem to notice. Instead, he focused his attention on me. "Look, Glory, I know it has to be upsetting. But this postcard doesn't really change anything."

"What do you mean?" I asked. "Rocky left Flat Falls and went to Panama City. My father might have already died when that postcard was sent."

His expression softened. "And how do you know that, exactly?"

"Look at the date!" I said, jabbing my finger into the desk. "It's from the year Rocky disappeared."

"And how many months were there in that year?"

I crossed my arms and offered him a petulant eye roll. "Twelve."

"Your parents were killed in early August." His gentle tone was almost my undoing. "So there were seven months before that where Rocky could have made a trip down South before the night in question."

"I know that, but…" My hope plummeted. "He didn't do it. Surely there's a way to figure out the exact date this was sent—some sort of forensic ink examination."

My voice was much smaller than it should have been, given the amount of bravado I'd felt when I stalked past the receptionist a few minutes earlier. "I've got something the chief is going to want to see," I had said with a breezy finger wave. "And I'm here to prove a man's innocence."

Hollis leaned forward, and his chair let out a groan of frustration that echoed the one that was building in my chest. "We might never know exactly what happened, but the investigators have met with all the witnesses from the night of the fight, and they feel confident in marking the case closed."

"Who? Who are these witnesses?" I asked, grasping at the last few straws of my dignity before I lost all control of myself and started blubbering in the middle of the police station.

"No. I don't know what you're planning, but the answer is a firm no."

"I just want to know who they are, Hollis," I insisted. "I'm not going to interrogate them at gunpoint or toilet paper their houses."

He released a sigh. "Only because it's public record, I will ask the investigator to provide you with a list of names. But you are not, under any circumstances, to do any investigative work on your own. That's why we have a team of trained detectives."

I agreed with a dip of my chin, mentally crossing my fingers behind my back so I didn't feel badly when I showed up on the so-called witnesses' doorsteps.

"I am glad that you stopped by, though," Hollis added. "You've saved me a trip."

"Was there something else you wanted to talk to me about?" I asked.

"Not you," he replied, shifting in his seat. "Ian." Hollis flipped open the lid of his laptop and clicked a few keys. "Word on the street is that you had a beef with Burton Levi."

Ian's expression didn't change, but the muscles in his forearms bunched up as he gripped the arms of the chair. "I did."

"Care to tell me about it?" Hollis asked.

I tapped my hand on the desk. "Does he need an attorney for this conversation?"

Hollis stared at Ian for a heartbeat too long before finally responding. "No. I'm simply asking a longtime Flat Falls resident to give me a little background on an outsider who was found dead in a freezer in the middle of my town."

"Didn't he just fall and hit his head?" I asked.

"The autopsy results aren't back yet," Hollis replied. "But Wayne Daly has been calling my office three times a day to see if we've arrested anybody yet."

"And have you?" Ian asked.

Hollis shook his head. "Chief Daly seems to have a particular interest in the members of our restaurant community, and I figured there's nobody better to give us a rundown of the perils one can find in the kitchen than Ian here."

Ian crossed his arms in front of his chest. "Kitchens can be dangerous places."

Hollis's raised brow issued a challenge. "Do you have someone who can verify your whereabouts before and during Ruby's wedding luncheon?"

I leaped up, spurred on by a dangerous combination of adrenaline and indignation. "You can't possibly think—"

Ian held out his palm. "It's fine, Glory. I have nothing to hide. Yes, I was at Trolls all afternoon. We had a water leak in the bar, and I spent the better part of the day making sure the plumber didn't get too friendly with the beer taps the way he did the last time he paid us a visit."

"You didn't plan on coming to the luncheon?" Hollis asked.

"Not a chance."

Hollis tapped his pen on the edge of his desk. "And why is that?"

Ian leaned forward, bringing his gaze level with Hollis's. "Because Burton Levi was an arrogant son-of-a—" He broke off. "That was my contract, and I was furious at the mayor for yanking it away from me. If you're asking if I killed him, the answer is no. But just because I'm not the one who pulled the trigger doesn't mean I'm upset that he's gone."

17

———

Beverlee and I had been working all afternoon to ensure that every single detail of Ruby and Warren's wedding the next day would be perfect. The bridesmaids were tucked away at the Flat Falls Day Spa getting warm rocks rubbed all over their backs, which Beverlee assured me was an incredibly relaxing way to spend the day.

I told her it didn't matter if they were tattooing donkeys on their faces if it kept them out of my hair.

Even Warren was accounted for. He had visited my office earlier to pick up his tux, which the tailor had delivered that morning, and spent almost ten minutes promising me he memorized the schedule and would be waiting at the altar on time the next afternoon.

"And Ruby's dress? Where do we stand with getting it restored to wedding-ready condition?" I asked as Beverlee went through the to-do list in preparation for the big day.

"Delivered to the mayor's house this morning," she answered. "And from what I hear, Moe couldn't stop unzipping the garment bag to sneak a peek. He apparently cried three times before the delivery girl could leave."

While I was thrilled for Ruby that her father would be there to walk her down the aisle, the father-daughter dynamic was often the hardest part of a wedding day for me. Unlike Ruby, who had picked out the song for the father-daughter dance before the wedding planning had even started, I'd walked down the aisle without my dad.

I cleared my throat and pushed back from the conference room table. "It looks like we've got everything under control for tomorrow. Even the weather is cooperating."

North Carolina weather in the spring was tempestuous at best, but we appeared to be in store for a perfectly clear day with little wind. That was good news for the crew Moe hired to spend their morning weaving wisps of tulle and strings of globe lights along the waterfront.

"Then we're free to enjoy the festival this afternoon," Beverlee replied. "I hear there's going to be a fire juggling demonstration by the local high school performing arts troupe. If it's anything like last year, we'll get to watch all the firefighters scurry around trying to extinguish the foliage. And if you get flushed, they bring you water and check your vitals." She fanned her face with a stack of paper.

Only Beverlee would turn the incineration of public property into both a spectator event and a dating opportunity.

~

THE FESTIVAL WAS in full swing when we stepped outside. Children streaked by with colorful balloon animals shaped like dolphins and giraffes while their parents munched on popcorn and hot dogs smeared with ketchup and mustard. Live beach music blared through oversized speakers, and the early afternoon sun gave everything a magical, golden radiance.

"Shall we find the firefighters?" Beverlee suggested while she topped off her lipstick in the reflection of a parking meter.

I was just about to give in when Scoots came tearing out of the pawnshop. "Did he find you?"

"Who?" I asked.

"Chief Daly. He came to Flat Falls to ask you more questions about the body you found under Big River Earl. And he might have also mentioned a citation for driving away from him the other day."

"I'm not in the mood to be interrogated about dead people or traffic violations tonight."

She gave an understanding nod. "That's why I sent him toward the food carts. Told him the last time I saw you, you were knee-deep in a frozen lemonade."

"Good thinking," Beverlee said. "The stage is in the opposite direction."

The three of us headed toward the stage with Beverlee craning her neck every few seconds to monitor for flames that would require attention from a first responder.

I bobbed my head to the upbeat music as we walked. Out of the corner of my eye, I caught a flash of movement, and I whipped around to find Wayne Daly shoving his way through the crowd. He waved his arms like a hyperactive jellyfish as he dodged ice cream cones and dancing teenagers.

The entire time, his gaze stayed locked on mine.

"He's here," I said to Beverlee. "We've got to go."

I clutched Beverlee's wrist, and she hooked a hand around Scoots's bicep. We snaked our way through the throng of people, finally making it to a clearing in the parking lot outside an abandoned warehouse on the edge of the waterfront district.

The warehouse had sat mostly empty for the last few years, except for a minor stint as a sound stage for a reality show that had evolved into a wedding disaster. During this year's festival, though, it had been transformed into a funhouse. Bright flags danced in the breeze, and a disco light splattered bursts of color on the metal walls. A hand-painted sign promising family fun for five dollars a person leaned up against a folding table, and Shirley from the Grind and Go manned the cash box.

I glanced over my shoulder and saw that the chief had almost broken through the crowd. With no time to spare, I yelled, "In here!" and scrambled around the entry table and into the warehouse with Scoots at my side.

"Where's Beverlee?" My heart pounded in tune with the flashing lights and techno music.

"I'm right here," she said, bursting through the door. "I had to pay for our tickets."

"We're not here for fun, Beverlee," I replied. "We're trying to get away from the cops."

She threw up her hands. "You see? That's what's wrong with young people these days. Always trying to get around the rules."

Scoots elbowed her way between us. "Are we just going to stand here and chatter all night, or are we going to get moving? Wayne is going to follow us in here at any minute."

I gave Beverlee a final petulant scowl before motioning toward the hall of mirrors. "There's an air vent on the other side of the warehouse. The metal slides away, and you can get out of the building without being seen."

She didn't ask how I knew that, which was good, since I didn't want to admit that I had spent a good portion of my teenage years hiding from the world within these very walls.

"I'm not sure I like this," Beverlee said as she and Scoots followed me into the maze of mirrors. "It's not good for anyone to see their thighs this many times."

I had to agree. Beverlee glared at me from dozens of positions around the room.

"Let's just find that vent," Scoots said. "I want to get out of here so I can get some chili fries."

She marched forward and smacked her face into a mirror. The resulting curse didn't require any sort of amplification; it echoed through the room all on its own.

"Follow me," I said, holding my palm out in front of my face. I felt along the walls until I came to an open panel and dragged Beverlee by her wrist through the opening. Instead of an escape route, though, we were met with more mirrors.

Just then, the lights flickered off, then blasted back on in a frenzy of colors. Scoots barreled into me, her fingernails digging into my shoulder. "Are they trying to make us puke?"

I didn't have a chance to respond before the lights dimmed again. Only this time, when they turned back on, Chief Daly's face appeared in the center of about a dozen mirrors.

"Glory Wells," he called. "Stay where you are. I need to speak with you."

"I don't think so," Beverlee muttered, shuffling her feet on the concrete floor and kicking at the mirrors to find the openings.

The chief was gaining ground, but the three of us stumbled and crashed our way through the set until we made it to the next opening. But instead of mirrors, the next room featured an oversized ball pit flanked by a gang of clowns.

I had always firmly believed that there are two types of

people in the world: people who hate clowns with a fiery passion and liars. So when the first clown stepped toward me with a painted-on grin and a full head of curly neon hair, I did the only thing I could.

I punched her.

My fist landed squarely on the pink circles that dotted her cheeks, and she stumbled backward into a black curtain. When she reached out to steady herself, the entire wall and its metal supports came clattering down in a barrage of balls and curses.

The clown straightened her wig and scrambled up from the floor. "Dang it, Glory. What was that for?"

"Maggie?" I asked, recognizing the town's other wedding planner. I stopped to admire her bulbous red nose and oversized polyester jumpsuit, but Scoots dragged me over the curtain before I could dig my phone out of my pocket to take a snapshot for my memory book.

Two other clowns tried righting the curtains while Maggie bellowed, her hands clenched into fists as the floor undulated with colorful balls. I kicked them out of my way as I made my way toward the back of the warehouse.

Just before I pried the sheet metal back to help Scoots and Beverlee slide through the vent opening to freedom, I turned around and tossed Maggie a satisfied smirk.

Maybe being chased by the cops wasn't such a bad thing, after all.

WE WERE STILL LAUGHING when we tumbled through the door to my apartment a few minutes later.

"Do you think we could talk one of the food trucks into delivering?" Scoots asked. "I'm going to be upset if hiding from the law means I can't have nachos for dinner."

"I'll go get your food," Beverlee answered, turning toward me. "Do you want anything, Glory?"

I had come down from the high of evading Wayne Daly, and the impact of being questioned as part of a murder investigation settled onto my chest.

"I'm going to pass," I replied. "I'm not hungry."

Beverlee pressed her palm against my forehead. "Are you ill?"

I shook my head. "No, I'm just thinking."

She studied me for a moment. "Are you still worrying about your dad?"

"How could I not? Hollis said they'll be closing the investigation soon, and I failed him."

Beverlee gathered me in a tight hug. "You didn't fail him, honey."

After a moment of letting myself get lost in her embrace, I stepped back, lifting my arms in frustration. "I feel like I'm missing something."

"I don't see what. You've been through all the evidence you could get your hands on, which wasn't much."

"That's just it," I replied, frustration growing inside my chest. "We had all these pieces of the puzzle, but they just don't fit."

"Maybe they never will," she added softly. "And that's okay. Even if we figured out who killed Rocky, it wouldn't bring your parents back."

I swiped a single tear as it rolled down my cheek. "I wish I still had that box from Ada's house. Whoever took it thought it was important enough to break into my office to steal from me."

"What about the other one, then?" Scoots suggested from her perch on my sofa. "You mentioned there was a second box in Ada's closet."

"Ada denied that it was important."

Beverlee crossed her arms in front of her chest. "I know she's your grandma, baby, but do you really trust her to tell you the truth?"

I considered her question for a moment and shook my head. "No, I don't."

"Then there's your answer," she said. "You need to make sure there's nothing important in that other box."

I turned the idea over in my head for half a second, then pivoted and determinedly snatched my keys off the table. "I'll be back in an hour."

"You're going now?" Beverlee asked, glancing out the window. "Do you want me to come with you?"

"I don't think so," I replied. "I won't be gone long. I'm just going to have a brief chat with my grandmother to find out what she has been hiding from me."

18

———

"No," Ada replied, finally opening the door to my repeated banging. "You cannot come in."

I leaned against the front porch column, hoping the rotten wood would hold my weight. "Why not?" I asked. "Isn't a woman allowed to come visit her grandmother?"

Ada inspected me as if she had just found a squished slug in her breakfast cereal. "I don't have any interest in talking to you."

I guess any connection we had forged while stealing trash the day before had disappeared. "Come on, Ada. I just want to talk."

She scowled.

"Grandmother?" I asked, forcing a sweet smile.

Her scowl deepened.

"Granny?" I tried, scrolling through the thesaurus in my brain to come up with some term of endearment that would build a bridge between us.

"I don't have time for this." She stepped back to close the door.

But considering that it had taken me ten minutes of

beating on that same door to persuade her to open it in the first place, I wasn't about to let her slam it without a fight.

"Listen," I said with a heavy sigh. "They're about to close the case. They think Daniel killed Rocky."

Ada's shuffling stilled.

"Ada," I said, dropping my voice to almost a whisper. "Do you think that's what happened?"

She gave a harsh grunt. "You lost your chance to help me. I don't want to talk about my boys with you anymore."

"And why not?" I asked, suddenly feeling emboldened by the memory of my father. He would have wanted me to find out the answers. He would have wanted me to figure out who killed his brother.

"Because you look like her," Ada spat.

"Like who? My mother?"

"Like the woman who took my Daniel away," she replied, her scowl replaced with haunted resignation.

With her sunken cheeks and pursed lips, Ada Boyd suddenly looked every bit of her eighty-one years.

I reached out to comfort her, but she swatted my hand away. "So get lost."

"I want to help you figure out what happened."

She glanced over my shoulder and lifted a bony finger. "Then you should start with him."

I followed her gaze to her neighbor, Bud, who was trimming a bush on the back of his property with hand clippers.

"Bud Perkins?" I asked. "What does he have to do with this?"

"Everything. You've been so busy getting cozy with him, but did you ever think to ask him what he was doing the night your parents died?"

"Bud?" I repeated. "He didn't know my parents."

"Maybe not," she replied with a smug smile. "But he was driving the truck that killed them."

I STOOD on my grandmother's empty front porch while time swirled around me. Everything faded away as I descended the stairs and strode across Ada's barren lawn toward Bud.

Phil Donahue, who was lounging in the shade next to him, scrambled out when he saw me approach, but I didn't even acknowledge him.

My focus was only on Bud.

Friend.

Neighbor.

Murderer.

He greeted me as I approached. "Hey, Glory. What brings you to our neck of the woods today?"

"Is it true?" I asked, struggling to keep my voice steady. "Were you driving the truck that killed my parents?"

He set the clippers on the ground next to him and slowly slipped off his gardening gloves and lifted his gaze to meet mine. "Yes."

My head fell into my hands as I collapsed onto his wrought iron garden bench. "Why didn't you tell me?"

Bud eased himself onto the seat next to me. "I didn't know who you were at first. And by the time I figured it out, there wasn't an easy way for me to slip it into conversation."

Betrayal rose in my throat. "You should have tried."

He dropped his chin but said nothing.

By then, the tears I had been holding in for days—decades, even—had broken free. Within seconds, I moved past gentle weeping and into full ugly cries. My breaths came hard and fast, and once my sleeves were soaked, I mopped up the tears with the hem of my shirt.

Bud still didn't speak. Instead, he sat with my grief as if it was his own. And maybe it was.

I wiped my cheek again with the sleeve that I had clenched in my fist. "Beverlee always said it was an accident. And I never asked for any details, because she said that accidents don't point fingers. All I know is that they were on the bridge, and a semi-truck came out of nowhere. That was you. You're the one who hit their car and knocked them over the side and into the water."

He slid his glasses off slowly, and for the first time, I noticed his eyes had filled with unshed tears. He took his time wiping the lenses with a rag from his pocket before placing them carefully back on his face.

I expected him to defend himself, or at least provide me with a litany of excuses about why it happened. He was driving too fast. There was an animal on the road. His brakes failed.

But he didn't. Instead, he patiently waited for me to move through my grief until I was ready to ask him the question I had been avoiding for years. "What happened?"

Bud cleared his throat and watched Phil peck around in the dirt for a moment before he responded. "It was a long shift. An accident on I-40 outside of Raleigh had backed traffic up for hours, and I was ready to be home."

I scrubbed a circle in the dirt with my toe while I waited for him to continue.

"There was always this moment, just before the bridge came into view, where I'd get a sense of relief. No matter how long my haul was, I knew I was home."

I could relate to the feeling. I had always felt the same way when I pulled up to Beverlee's bungalow. It was like the rest of the world's worries faded away, and I was safe.

"That day was no different," Bud continued, digging into his shirt pocket for a handful of seeds, which he tossed into the mulch. Phil came running, his cheerful chatter a sharp contrast to the sadness on his owner's face. "And even though I was late, I knew Betty had kept supper warm for me. She always made pot roast when I came home from a long run." A smile flitted across his face at the memory. "She said it was worth celebrating, and she'd put out the good china and make me use a cloth napkin."

"That sounds nice," I admitted. I watched as he lost himself in memories and fought my impatience for information. For answers.

"It was. But that night, something was different. The road wasn't clear." His voice picked up its pace, and his tone was clipped.

"Why?" I asked, desperate for answers that I wasn't sure he even had.

Bud shook his head. "That's the thing, Glory, I can't remember. Everything from before the accident until I woke up in the hospital just… disappeared. The doctors said that was normal after a head trauma."

I jumped up from the bench and stalked away, causing Phil Donahue to flap his wings and screech. Then I whirled back around to face Bud, anger and frustration bubbling inside me. "You don't remember anything? Like how there was a car on the road, and how you killed two innocent people?"

His shoulders slumped. "I filled in the pieces for the investigators the best I could, Glory. But it was dark, and late, and… I just don't know."

I crossed my arms in front of me. "I want to know why they didn't charge you," I said, my voice raw.

"The investigators determined I wasn't at fault," he replied, his knuckles white from clutching at the back of the bench. "But aside from the notes they took from a rambling man with a head injury at the accident scene, I don't have anything else to tell you. I'm sorry."

"What kind of notes?"

He rose and motioned for me to follow him toward the house. "I've got a copy of the report if you want to see it. Maybe it will help you find the closure you're looking for."

"It was twenty-five years ago, and you still have the report?" I asked. "Why?"

He didn't even look at me when he answered. "Next to the day my Betty died, it was the worst day of my life."

At least we had that much in common.

"I'd like to see it," I whispered.

He nodded and slipped inside the house.

I don't know why I hadn't asked to see the actual report over the years. I had heard about the accident since I was in kindergarten, and I always thought that the platitudes and condolences from nearly everyone in Flat Falls had given me all the information I needed. One day my parents were here, lifting me high in the air between our joined hands as we walked along the beach.

And the next day they were gone.

Moments later, he returned with a few sheets of paper, yellowed along the edges and stapled together. "There's not much here, I'm afraid. But you're welcome to them if they would help."

I took the papers from him with trembling fingers and scanned the contents. "You told the police there was a woman in the road."

My mother.

"Like I said, my memories of the accident are spotty. But I remember seeing someone and swerving to avoid hitting her."

I ran my fingers along the words on the report as if they would help connect me to her.

"I'm sorry, Glory," Bud said, letting out a shaky breath that seemed to carry decades of worry and remorse. "I'm so very sorry."

"Did Beverlee know?" I asked, conspiracy theories already forming in my mind. "Did she keep it from me all these years?"

He shook his head and extended a shaky finger toward the police report. "I don't think so. Most people back then knew me as William. I was only Bud to my family and friends."

"Wasn't it all over the news, though?" I pressed my knuckles into my temple. "Beverlee wouldn't have just let something like that go."

He let out a mirthless chuckle and pulled his phone from his back pocket, letting it drop onto the bench. "It was before we carried the Internet in our pants. She probably didn't make the connection."

"What about Ada? She couldn't have thought it was a coincidence that you moved in next door."

He cast a quick glance toward my grandmother's house. "It actually *was* a coincidence. I lived here for three years before she got one of my seed catalogs in error. She recognized my name and delivered it to my front porch wrapped around a clump of dog poop she scraped off the sidewalk. It took me a few days to figure out who would give me such an unusual housewarming gift."

An incredulous laugh bubbled out before I could stop it. That seemed like something Ada would do.

Bud and I sat in silence for a while as I digested the news. I wanted to make sense of it all. To lash out, pounding my fists into his chest to fill the deep hole that had taken up residence in my own. But the truth was that I liked Bud Perkins, and there had been more going on that night than just a simple accident.

My father had been fighting with his brother before he died. Surely that wasn't a coincidence. There had to be more evidence that could help me figure out what happened that night.

I took in Bud's drawn features, noting the shadows underneath his eyes.

I needed answers for myself. And for Bud, too. He had spent so many years blaming himself for my parents' death. And maybe he was responsible.

But maybe he wasn't.

I needed to get my hands on that second box.

I shifted my gaze over to my grandmother's house just as her paper curtains fluttered closed. "Why this house? If it wasn't because of Ada, what made you decide to move in here?" I asked.

Bud looked up in surprise. "My kids said I was getting crotchety wandering the halls where Betty and I built our life together, and I agreed it was time for a fresh start. The exact house didn't seem important since she wasn't here to enjoy it with me, so this place was as good as any."

"So you two have never been friendly?"

His brow crept up, but his expression didn't change. "We're neighbors, not friends."

I nodded slowly, a plan taking shape inside my head.

"I'm not ready to forgive you yet," I said. "But how do you feel about a little neighborly breaking and entering?"

"It depends," he replied, his hand reaching out to mine. "Are felonies the gateway to forgiveness?"

19

————

Bud fed me peanut butter and celery at his kitchen island while we debated the best way to get into Ada's house.

"Why don't you just ask her for the box?" he suggested.

"She already said no," I replied. "Twice."

"Then maybe you should just leave it—"

I snapped a piece of celery with my teeth. "No. I need to know what's in there and why she gets so shifty about it. I think she knows more about what happened that day than she's letting on."

Bud pressed his thumbs into his eyebrows while he considered my request. "Okay, I'll make you a deal."

I licked peanut butter off my fingertip. "I'm listening."

"I'll help you."

"If?"

"If you'll put a good word in for me with one of your lady friends."

"With Beverlee?" I scoffed. "You don't need me for that. She's practically waiting by the phone for you to call as we speak."

He shook his head. "No, not with Beverlee. With Scoots."

I practically fell off the metal barstool. "I knew it! I told Beverlee you were giving Scoots sugar eyeballs, but she insisted that wasn't possible because Scoots is…"

"Smart? Strong?" He narrowed his eyes in a challenge.

"Sure," I replied. "Let's go with that."

"She reminds me of my Betty, and there's not a day that goes by that I don't miss that sass."

Scoots had been a second mother to me, balancing out Beverlee's pie-in-the-sky parenting with her patented, no-nonsense charm. I warmed inside at the thought that someone else recognized it, too.

I gave him a small smile. "You don't have to help me break into Ada's house, Bud. I'll still put in a good word for you."

And that was all it took. He slid onto a kitchen chair with a resigned sigh. "I'm not going to break the law. That Chief Daly is an unruly fellow, and I try to steer clear of him."

I assured him that he was safe from Wayne and that all he needed to do was help me get Ada out of the house for a few minutes so I could sneak in and grab the box.

"I'll move my car over to Wilton Street, so she doesn't know I'm still here. And then you can distract her for a few minutes in your garden while I swoop in. Easy breezy."

He cast a doubtful glance out his kitchen window. "How am I supposed to get her out of the house? I always assumed Ada was going to be one of those people who needed to be extricated by crane when she passes."

I hid my snort behind my knuckles. "Well, we've had an emotional day over here. Maybe our conversation left you wanting to make amends for what happened all those years ago."

He pondered my suggestion. "It could work…"

I slid my gaze around his almost-bare countertops. "Do you have anything you could take as a peace offering? Like a plant or a jar of apple butter?"

Beverlee always said there was no sin large enough that a handmade gift couldn't make it right. She had spent more than three days stewing apples with sticks of cinnamon for the entire science department at my high school after I set the lab on fire. I'd been too busy flirting with Ian to notice the flame from my Bunsen burner getting close to Trinity Lockman's over-sprayed French braids.

It wasn't my fault that she freaked out at a tiny bit of smoke and dumped her beaker of isopropyl alcohol on it— nor was it my fault that the teenager-sized fireball happened to be right next to the stack of brand-new chemistry textbooks.

She was fine, thank goodness, but the scent of cinnamon still made me feel a twinge of guilt.

"I don't have anything to give her," Bud said, "except a handful of birdseed or a half-eaten burrito left over from last night."

I almost asked for the burrito for myself but decided against it. Instead, I eyed the loaf of bread on the counter. It was cheap sliced multigrain from the bargain bin at the deli counter, but it would have to do. "Got any ribbon?"

HALF AN HOUR LATER, Bud walked me to my car, and I made a show of hugging him extra tight.

Take that, Ada. I don't have to hold a grudge for decades.

But Bud smelled like spicy aftershave, his navy cardigan was soft against my cheek, and his strong arms felt the way I'd always imagined a grandfather's would, so I curled my fingers against his back and stayed there for a few heartbeats longer.

When I pushed away, I gave him a quick thumbs-up. "I'd say I owe you one, but we both know that's not true."

His lips turned upward in a wry smile. "If I end up in jail because of this, I'm never going to forgive you."

I tossed him a wink before sinking into the front seat and starting the car. "I'd be giving you another reason to call on Scoots. You know she used to be a lawyer, right?"

I parked a street over and hid behind a wax myrtle across from Ada's house while he gathered his loaf of bread, which from the looks of it, he had wrapped with a big red bow he'd pulled off his Christmas wreath.

Finally, he made his way to Ada's front door and knocked.

She ignored him.

He cast an uncertain glance over his shoulder and knocked again.

I released a whoosh of breath when she finally inched the door open. Her voice was loud enough to carry across the lawn.

"What do you want?" she asked.

"I brought bread," Bud replied, sticking the paper bag through the opening. "A peace offering."

When she didn't immediately reach out to take it, I worried she would turn him down and slam the door in his face. But after a moment, she snatched the package.

"We have a lot to talk about," Bud said. "And I was hoping you'd join me in my garden for a few minutes."

"Why would I want to do that?" Ada eyed him suspiciously.

Bud swept his hand across the yard. "It's a beautiful day, and I always find that fresh air helps clear out the cobwebs.

And besides, Phil Donahue is getting his exercise, so I need to keep an eye on him."

Ada poked her head out the door and eyeballed the chicken as he bounced around the yard. She grumbled something about old men and their odd pets, but she let him lead her across the grass.

After he got her seated on the bench with her back angled away from her front door, Bud flashed me a thumbs-up and a wide grin, which he transformed into a solemn frown as he settled himself on the bench next to her.

The *Mission Impossible* theme song played in my head as I bounded up the front stairs and slipped into Ada's house, but as soon as I shut the door behind me, my heart thundered.

The room was mostly dark, and the dust dancing in the little streams of light filtering through the gap between the newspapers made me want to use my T-shirt as a respirator. I wondered how someone could sit in the dark all day, surrounded by frozen food boxes, diet soda cans, and decades' worth of memories?

My father took his first steps here. Did his homework. Got ready for his first date.

I glanced at a portrait on the wall and recognized his smile easily. He was dressed in white pants and a light blue button-up shirt, an Easter basket on the ground in front of him. At his side sat a toddler whose face was smeared with the remains of a chocolate bunny he held within his chubby grip. The boys grinned at each other. How old were they when their relationship fell apart?

A wave of sadness washed over me that I couldn't do my father the honor of straightening out the crooked frame or cleaning off the grime. Instead, I kissed the tips of my fingers and pressed them to the glass.

"Love you."

In response, I heard Ada's voice drifting back toward the house. "I ain't got time for this. My soap is about to come on."

Panic flashed inside my chest as I whirled toward the closet. I'd wasted precious seconds getting sentimental and was about to pay the price.

I flung open the bi-fold door, wincing when it got stuck in its tracks. I jerked it hard, and my jaw dropped when the top connector came loose, leaving the door swinging free instead of attached at the top.

I stretched up and groped along the top of the door. Finding the spring, I pressed it in while wiggling the door along the track.

It was a trick I'd learned at Beverlee's. Her pantry door used to come loose just like that, and if I wanted a snack after hiding half of the kale salami surprise she had cooked for dinner, I had to get in and out quickly.

When the door clicked back into place, I let out a whoosh of breath. I slid it open carefully, almost squealing with joy when the box I wanted was right where I hoped it would be.

I grabbed it, tucked it under my arm, and pivoted toward the door.

But just as I rounded the corner toward freedom and sunlight, Ada's voice sounded on the porch.

"Why are you following me?" she called. "Are you making a pass?"

"It's just so important for us to make amends, Ada." Bud was yelling, and I could picture Ada's annoyed scowl even before she replied.

"It's fine," she said. "But you're not my type."

The handle rattled, and I dove behind her recliner just as the front door swung open.

Ada shuffled into the room and moved to close it

behind her. But Bud had stopped it from closing, and from my hiding place behind the chair, I could just make out the toe of his white leather sneaker peeking over the threshold.

"Oh, please," he cried, throwing himself against the wood door with a loud thud. "I need to hear you say that you forgive me."

And with that, he shoved his way into the living room and executed a Shakespeare-worthy swoon onto the sofa.

I leaned my head out from behind the recliner and caught his gaze.

"Mr. Perkins." Ada's voice rose in frustration. "You need to leave."

"Of course, of course." He attempted to push himself up from the overstuffed seat. "I just get so overcome with emotion. I'm sure you understand."

He let out a loud gasp, which he covered by clutching his chest and wailing in earnest.

"What... do you need some sort of help?" Ada asked him.

"No, but a glass of water might be nice," he replied, followed by a dramatic hiccup.

She wandered into the kitchen, and I scrambled out from behind the chair.

"Go," Bud mouthed, pointing to the door.

I made a run for it. And the last thing I heard as I turned the street corner was Bud's voice calling out cheerfully, "Never mind, Ada. I'm just going to head home. Lovely chatting with you."

I WAITED until my heart rate returned to normal before pulling into a drug store parking lot. I lifted the lid of the cardboard box and slid it gently onto the seat next to me.

Much like the box of Rocky's things, this one was filled almost to the top with memories. I ran my palm along a red ribbon that said Second Place, Big River Elementary Spelling Bee.

I chuckled, doubting Daniel Boyd was happy about coming in second. We had that in common. I was still bitter that Maggie had beaten me in the elementary spelling bee.

Next, I drew out a small photo album, the spine cracking when I opened it. Inside were pictures from my parents' small courthouse wedding. Mom looked lovely in a white lace column dress, a spray of wildflowers clutched in her hands. Beside her, my father stood tall in a dark gray suit, his beard trimmed short and a single red rose pinned to his lapel.

They looked young. Happy.

My stomach lurched at the thought that they'd be gone a mere five years later.

I flipped through the photo album, my eyes watering at the sight of Beverlee catching the bouquet. Ada appeared to be frowning through the whole ceremony, and through every image, Rocky stood next to Daniel with a scowl.

Beneath the photo album, a folded navy jacket cushioned a high school diploma and a pair of bronzed baby shoes. I traced the cold metal, wondering what Ada was like as a young mother. Did she play games with her boys? Bake them cookies? Was she the type to sit in the front row of every performance? I couldn't envision it, but then again, I hadn't expected the framed Easter portrait. I couldn't imagine how it felt to be a single mother raising two boys alone. Did her bitterness stem from her loss, or was it always there, part of her family's fabric?

At the very bottom of the box sat a stack of photos tied with a frayed pink ribbon. When I slipped the ribbon off, I recognized a picture from my first day of kindergarten.

Unlike a lot of days from my early childhood, I remembered that one clearly. I had a new yellow backpack with a matching Care Bears lunch box, and my hair was tied back in bouncy pigtails. White socks folded over at my ankles, and my pale blue plaid dress hadn't yet met the perils of the Flat Falls Elementary playground or a little girl who liked to make mud pies and play with marsh frogs.

I looked happy and proud, and except for the large bandage on my right knee, courtesy of an unsuccessful attempt to reach Beverlee's roof via the live oak tree in her garden, the photo could have easily passed as an advertisement for the picture-perfect first day of school.

That wasn't the only photo of me. There were images of me splashing at the beach and blowing out the candles on my third birthday cake, and along with a snapshot of my mom with her head resting on Dad's shoulder, they presented the image of an idyllic little family.

Several of them were taken after my parents' death, which led me to the question: how had Ada gotten her hands on them?

I got that answer when I located an envelope bearing Beverlee's return address and elegant cursive script. Apparently, in Beverlee's endless optimism, she had been including Ada in my life despite her animosity.

At the bottom of the stack, there was a single photo of my parents. My father's palm rested gently on her rounded belly, and his wide grin was focused solely on his wife. Rocky sat in the center of the group, his right hand lifted toward the camera in a wave.

Several friends surrounded them on the sand, and the atmosphere appeared festive. Beverlee sported a big grin and a wide-brimmed sun hat as she raised a champagne toast, the Fowlers reclined beneath an oversized beach umbrella, and Shirley from the Grind and Go grinned around a marshmallow she was nibbling off a skewer fresh from the bonfire.

The only person who didn't look relaxed was Burton Levi. He leaned against a boulder and watched his wife dancing beside the fire, arms raised.

Virginia wore a short pink sundress that flared out as she twirled, her long hair wild and stacks of bangle bracelets and long necklaces reflecting the light from the fire.

She was radiant. Carefree.

But something had changed her, and there was only one person who could tell me what that was.

Ruby and Warren had decided to forego the traditional rehearsal dinner in favor of an intimate picnic on the beach, but I knew Warren's mother was still running around finalizing last-minute details.

A quick text from Beverlee informed me that Virginia had headed back to the library to grab some family photos to display at the ceremony in honor of her husband. The clock on the Mustang's dashboard said I had ten minutes until the library closed, which was just enough time for me to corner her behind a stack of cookbooks and ask about my parents.

When I pulled into the parking lot, the sky danced in swirls of pink and orange, and the town workers in the library's municipal complex had already begun their weekend exodus away from desk jobs and toward the freedom of the ocean.

I grabbed my purse and glanced around the parking lot. A frazzled-looking mom had pulled a quilt out in the empty spot next to her brown minivan for snack time, but only a few other cars remained.

The breeze chilled my arms, and before I exited the car, I reached back in to grab my father's jacket. I slipped my arms into the sleeves, pretending it was his arms wrapping around me.

I gave a kid who was aiming goldfish crackers at passersby like tiny cheese grenades an extra-wide berth as I scooted toward the library entrance.

When I opened the front door of the library, the same assistant from my last visit pushed her book cart over to greet me. "Just so you know, we're closing soon. And I've got a date with an accountant in an hour, so I don't have time to stick around."

"Sure. I won't be here for long. I was just hoping to catch Virginia. I heard she was here picking up some pictures for the wedding."

"She was here a little while ago, but she might have left while I was on the phone." She shrugged. "But I have to get these books back on the shelf before I get out of here. I'm not sure…"

"I'll shoot her a text to let her know I'm here, and I'll stay out of your way while you finish up. If I don't hear back from her in a few minutes, I'll let myself out," I assured her.

Her fingertips tapped the top of the book cart while she examined the large clock on the wall behind the circulation desk. Apparently realizing she was letting valuable minutes with her crimping wand and an industrial-sized bottle of hairspray slip away from her, she agreed, the cart's wheels squeaking as she hurriedly turned to the task of shelving the rest of the books.

I dropped my purse on the floor and settled onto a paisley stuffed chair in the reading nook, my feet tucked beneath me, and flipped through a magazine while I waited. When Virginia still hadn't responded to my text a few minutes later, I dropped the magazine on a table and made a beeline for the adult fiction section, thumbing through a post-apocalyptic adventure novel. I promised myself that I'd get a new library card after the wedding and envisioned an entire weekend of nothing but bubble baths and reading.

As I trailed my fingers along the books' spines, I noticed that the storage room door was ajar. Unable to resist the temptation to see what other secrets Virginia had documented in her private scrapbooks, I slipped inside and pulled the door closed behind me.

Streams of fading light through a high window in the corner bathed the room in a warm orange glow. More items had been stuffed in there since my last visit, and I almost tripped over a crate of out-of-date scientific journals as I wandered over to the shelf where Virginia kept her memory box. I slid it off the shelf and dropped it onto the table, pushing aside the microfiche reader and tape recorder to make room. "All right, Virginia. Help me figure out what I've been missing."

I fished out a stack of pictures, smiling as I recognized snapshots from Warren's first birthday party. He wore a diaper and had chocolate frosting smeared all over his mouth and chest as he devoured a triple-layer cake while his father watched with a proud grin.

A few images of vacations over the years showed Warren and Burton playing on the beach or building a snowman in front of a ski chalet, but Virginia was nowhere to be seen. I pawed through the box, pulling out photo after photo of Warren with his father and not finding a single one that captured his mom. It was like she wasn't even there.

Virginia Levi had more reason than anyone else to hate her husband. He was loud, disrespectful, and disinterested in her as a person. To him, she was invisible.

I reached the very last photo in the box. It was separate

from the others, tucked under the folded edge of her scrapbook like an afterthought… or a secret.

This photo was the only one that included Virginia, and in it, she was anything but invisible. She wore a confident, sultry smile, her face partially hidden behind a curtain of dark hair as she leaned in close to Rocky Boyd, who was scooping potato salad onto her paper plate. Their heads were almost touching, and her pinky rested casually on top of his as he gripped the edge of the buffet table.

I flipped the picture over in my fingers as thoughts of Rocky's death floated through my mind. What if this was the start of their affair—the beginning of the events that would eventually lead to both Rocky and Burton's deaths?

I stashed the photo into my jeans pocket, returned the box to the shelf, and headed toward the storage room door. But when I twisted the handle, it didn't budge. I remembered how tight the door had been when Virginia tried to unlock it. No wonder the library volunteer had left it ajar—she knew that if she closed it, it would stick.

I banged on the door with the back of my fist to get her attention. "Hello?" I shouted. "I'm still in here."

No answer.

I pounded my knuckles against the wood over and over until I could feel the force of it echoing in my teeth. "I'm locked in! Can somebody help me?"

I hadn't been in the storage room for more than a few minutes, but the volunteer must have thought I left, and in her hurry to rendezvous with the accountant, she didn't bother checking through the building for stragglers.

Leaning against the door, I remembered the days when I, too, would be getting ready for a beachside campfire and not locked in a closet with boxes full of literary junk. I could almost smell the scent of burning wood as memories flitted through my head.

Suddenly, a sharp crack sounded from near the window in the corner, and I screamed as an orange flame reached its fingers through the decayed wood and then retreated.

"Fire! Somebody help me!" I yelled until my voice was raw, but nobody was there to rescue me. I patted my back pocket for my phone so I could call for assistance but realized I had left it next to the chair in the reading nook.

I expected the shrill blast of a smoke alarm as the wisps of smoke began to fill the room, but the only sound I heard was my fear-filled shouts. Even though I shoved at the door again and again, it didn't budge.

My only chance was the window, but unless I could get up there quickly, the flames would overtake my only escape route. I stacked two cardboard boxes and climbed on top to try to reach it, but I wasn't tall enough. Surveying the room, my gaze finally landed on a rickety bookshelf in the corner.

I scraped it along the floor and aligned it beneath the window opening. I climbed onto the top shelf, crediting all those nights of sneaking out during my teen years for my ability to balance while white knuckling the weathered wood window frame.

I pressed my palm to the glass, relieved to discover that the flames hadn't yet reached the window and were instead dancing through the library's walls. I stretched to peer through the glass, hoping to catch the attention of a passerby who also happened to be an emergency rescue expert. Unfortunately, the parking lot had emptied, so my frantic pleas were futile. Even the minivan mom with her portable snack buffet had moved on.

Running my fingers along the edge of the window confirmed my suspicion that it was just for show. There was no secret hinge or magic escape button.

I hadn't broken a window since I was twelve and tried to impress the shortstop at a pickup baseball game in the parking lot next to my orthodontist's office. I told him I was a world-class hitter.

I wasn't. Instead, my palms were so sweaty that when I drew back, the bat somersaulted out of my grip and smashed through the picture window into Dr. Mann's waiting room.

I swore I'd never play baseball again, but as the smoke swirled around me, I would have loved to uncover a spare Louisville Slugger leaning against the storage room wall. Instead, all I found was a worn copy of *War and Peace*.

Mrs. Hightower, my high school English teacher, claimed that one day it would offer me something meaningful, so I sent her a moment of acknowledgement as I heaved it at the window. Unfortunately, all it did was bounce off the glass and land with a resounding thud on the floor. Not altogether different from what happened the first time I read it.

I descended from the top of the bookshelf to find some other way to break the window, and in my panic, my foot slipped, sending me tumbling backward in a flurry of wind-mill arms and uncoordinated legs. My shoulder slammed against the table, and more than one of the old machines went crashing to the ground. As I struggled to right myself, a deep voice cut through the darkness.

"Yo, man. It's Rocky. We need to talk."

"Hello?" I called out as I searched for my rescuer, coughing as I covered my face with the hem of my shirt.

But the voice continued, and I realized that when it fell, the tape recorder had landed face-down, activating the play button. The voice echoing through the storage room wasn't a rescue team, but a recording.

"Burton, are you there? This isn't funny—you need to pick up, man." After a few moments of silence, he continued. "Look, I'm sorry about the kid. I never meant for any of this to happen, but I need you to call me."

A long beep signaled the end of the message, and my stomach heaved as I put the pieces together and came to the only conclusion that made any sense: Rocky Boyd wasn't *my* father, he was Warren Levi's. And Burton knew it.

No wonder he had been so cold to his wife all these years; he knew she had been unfaithful. And whether it was Burton or Virginia who buried my uncle beneath Big River Earl, she had to have known the truth was going to come out once his body was discovered, so she killed her husband to keep him from revealing her secrets to the world.

Virginia Levi was a killer—and she was also the only one who knew I was waiting for her in the library.

Coughs racked my chest as a cloud of smoke obscured the ceiling. It circled the room, a living being, angrily breathing and moaning as it gobbled up the air. I dropped to the floor and belly-crawled toward the door.

The handle was hot, so I wrapped my hand in the hem of my father's jacket and twisted as I put the full force of my nacho-loving hips into getting it to budge. Miraculously, it slipped open a few inches. Smoke billowed in, but I persisted. I put a shoulder up against it and shoved as hard as I could.

Finally, the door opened wide enough for me to slip out. By then, the flames had enveloped the reading nook and were making their way through the first stack of shelves.

I didn't have much time before the whole collection went down, and Beverlee would have my hide if she knew I stood by and let a fire destroy this many books. She had a soft spot for pet rescue videos and regency romance heroes.

I spotted the bright red fire extinguisher on the other

side of the picture books, I rushed across the room to grab it. Pulling the pin, I swept the extinguisher across the flames, thankful that Beverlee had included fire safety training in my childhood cooking lessons. Apparently, it was the only lesson that stuck.

I stumbled to the circulation desk and dialed 911 with shaking hands.

A casual voice with a decidedly Southern drawl answered on the seventh ring. "911. Can you hold please?"

The mellow tones of smooth jazz reached my ears before I could even respond.

I stretched the handset to arm's length and eyed it, wishing I could summon the fire department with my eyes alone.

It didn't work.

With a resigned sigh, I plunked the phone to the desk. If all those hours of watching late-night crime documentaries had taught me anything, it was that they'd be able to trace the call and could come to the rescue of Beverlee's smoldering romance novels then.

Because I didn't have time to wait around for a fire-fighter parade. I had a killer to stop before she sullied my father's name forever.

THE SUN WAS below the horizon when I pushed through the library's emergency exit, my lungs burning as I sucked in gulps of air. I was breathing like I had just finished an hour-long cardio workout. But my only exercise these days was running across town for burritos, so I knew my lungs were saturated with smoke.

I would have to look up the symptoms of smoke inhalation poisoning when I got home. If it was anything like the problems after I ate three-day-old shrimp from the Food Barn's discount section, I wanted nothing to do with it.

I crossed the parking lot with one thing on my mind: call Hollis. If I could get him to meet me at the police station, I could fill him in on what Virginia had done, and he'd be able to yank Rocky's murder report right out of those investigators' hands before it was too late.

Since my phone was currently being barbecued along with the rest of my purse on the floor of the reading nook, I had no way to call for help. I reached into my father's jacket pocket for the car keys, but they were gone. I groaned when I realized they must have fallen out when I was somersaulting over furniture in the storage closet.

That's what I got for trying to be a superhero.

I glanced around the parking lot, hoping for a bored taxi driver. Or even a bicycle. But I was alone in the industrial complex, and the darkness was quickly surrounding me.

Just then, a streetlamp in the far corner of the parking lot flickered on, and a beam of light shone down like a beacon on a decrepit old food truck with three bacon strips emblazoned on the side.

I ran toward it. "Masha!" I screamed. "Can you help me? I'll buy as many waffle cakes as you want. I just need a ride back to Flat Falls."

But she didn't answer.

I searched around the building, hoping to find her, but she wasn't there.

I jumped in the truck and laid on the horn. If anything would bring an irritable Russian lady running, it was the tinny sound of a pig oinking through her car's speakers.

Panic shot through me at the thought that something

had happened to her. She may have been stiffer than a piece of old shoe leather, but she made a good breakfast.

When she didn't appear, my only choice was to go for help. I turned the key, and the truck rumbled to life with far more enthusiasm than I expected, given that it was probably older than me and still held the laundry chute from its former life as a dry-cleaning delivery truck.

I clapped my hand on the dashboard, muttering a pep talk to both the truck and myself. "Let's go save the world."

She didn't respond, but I imagined the extra rumble underneath the driver's seat was the car equivalent of agreement. Either that or the carburetor was about to die. If this beast even had a carburetor. I knew even less about what was under the hood of the truck than I did about driving it, which became more and more obvious as I tapped the gas and lurched up over the curb while fumbling with the headlights. In case Masha was still around, I screamed, "I'm just borrowing this. I'm not stealing it."

I wasn't sure if that would get me out of criminal charges if Wayne Daly hunted me down, but it couldn't hurt, and it was an emergency. Certainly, I'd get some leniency for that.

If I didn't end up with face-down in a ditch first.

But it turned out that driving a giant breakfast wagon wasn't all that different from driving a sports car, except that the sports car took corners without jugs of maple syrup smashing to the floor and rolling up between the seats.

The truck had more pickup than I expected, and I was bouncing along the causeway at a respectable forty miles-an-hour when I spotted the flashing sirens heading toward the library. I gave the firefighters a jaunty wave as they passed, thankful they'd make sure there wasn't too much damage. I made a mental note to have Hollis call them later to explain what had happened. It would sound better coming from someone in uniform instead of yoga pants and a t-shirt.

Adrenaline throbbed through my head, making my hands shake and my heart beat in tune with the hair band anthem blaring through the radio.

I tried to turn the music down, but the volume knob broke off in my fingers just before the windshield wipers started a frantic dance across the glass, and the horn let off a startling blast of oinks.

Fortunately, cars on the streets of Big River took a weaving, oinking, rusty pig truck seriously. They all moved out of my way, even if some of them shouted obscenities as they did it.

I breathed a sigh of relief as I made it to the lonely stretch of highway that led to the bridge between Big River and Flat Falls. The sky was dark, and as I eased down the middle of the road, the adrenaline buzzing through my veins faded to a muted kind of euphoria.

I had figured out who killed Rocky and Burton, escaped from certain death in a blazing library, and was successfully maneuvering a giant stolen truck down the highway like a boss.

Borrowed, I amended. A borrowed truck.

I hadn't stolen a car since high school when Garritt Smith dared me to take the principal's hot dog-colored station wagon for a joyride during our Homecoming pep rally.

Fortunately, the principal had terrible eyesight, and by the time he located his glasses, which were in his shirt pocket the whole time, the wienermobile had been returned to its parking spot beside the dumpsters in the staff parking lot.

Thankfully, most of my indiscretions occurred before the days of on-campus security and viral social media posting. Teenagers couldn't get away with anything these days.

I rubbed my hand along the dashboard, hoping law enforcement would be more lenient with a thirty-something truck thief.

21

I was mentally preparing my speech to Hollis, making a note to emphasize the dire nature of being stranded in the middle of nowhere while fearing for my life instead of the fact that I stole a food truck, when I came upon a rusted red pickup truck parked on the side of the road just before the bridge, its hazard lights flashing through the darkness.

I fumbled around for the blinker, and after shooting what appeared to be a half gallon of window cleaner in the opposite direction of the windshield, I managed to pull to the side of the road, relieved when I finally came to a clunking stop.

Totty Fowler hopped out of the truck and sprinted to my window. Her flip-flops smacked on the pavement. "Oh my goodness, Glory. I was on my way back from the florist in Big River to pick up the boutonnieres for the ceremony tomorrow, and I ran into a little trouble. People kept driving by and tooting their horns, but nobody stopped."

"Do you have your phone?" I asked. "I need to call Hollis, and I'm sure you'd like to request a tow truck."

She shook her head. "No. I was in such a rush to get out the door that I left it on top of the copier in Moe's office. That's why I was so excited to see that food truck bouncing up over the sidewalk like a rescue chariot. And here you are, my knight in not-so-shiny armor."

"I am so happy to see you, too," I said, pulling her in for a shaky hug. "You wouldn't believe the evening I've had."

"I had to coordinate my future son-in-law's waxing appointment," she replied with a snort. "He wanted to be ready for the honeymoon. Can you top that?"

I shuddered, picturing Warren Levi's furry pecs. "Unfortunately, I think I can."

She glanced over at the food truck, which was sitting on the shoulder near the edge of the bridge. I had lost a box of pancake mix out the back door when I stopped, and one of the headlights flickered on and off like the front of the car was winking. "I didn't know you were moonlighting on the bacon truck. If you're that desperate for money, sweetie, Moe and I can help."

Part of me wanted to let her toss me a twenty. A new car was going to be expensive, and if she wanted to donate to the cause, so be it. But then I remembered the reason I was driving the food truck to begin with, and hot panic swirled in my chest. "I'm not. It's…"

I debated spilling the whole tale to her, but decided it was better if I told Hollis first. The police chief got antsy when the gossip mill got the scoop before the cops did. "It's a long story."

"Do you want to tell me about it on the way home? I'm in a bit of a rush."

"Of course," I replied. "Do you have anything you need to grab from the truck before we go?"

"No," she replied. "Moe can come back out later and help me get everything. It might convince him to finally get that wretched pickup fixed."

When I reached into my dad's jacket pocket for Masha's keys, my knuckles banged into something hard inside the interior chest pocket. I dug around the jacket lining until I located a hidden zipper, and when I opened it, my fingertips brushed against a piece of cold metal.

I withdrew my hand and held a tarnished silver locket up to the headlight. My fingers skated over the familiar floral filigree top, and tears flooded my eyes when I flipped open the case.

Tears blurred my vision as I took in the picture, a grainy snapshot of three faces sandwiched together.

Mom. Dad. Me.

The locket had been in my father's jacket pocket all this time—and not clenched in my uncle's bony dead fist.

"What do you have there?" Totty asked, angling her head to get a better look at the necklace.

"It's something that belonged to my mother," I replied.

I held it out to her, and she pressed her knuckles to her lips. "Oh my. That brings back some memories. Your mama loved that necklace."

I ran my thumb over it, a lump forming in my throat. "I remember."

"You can't really appreciate the love between a mother and a daughter until you have a baby of your own." She gave my shoulder a gentle squeeze. "And I can't believe my baby girl is getting married tomorrow. It seems like just yesterday her daddy was holding her up to the delivery room window for both of our families to see."

I could imagine the proud smile on Moe's face. Ruby had always been his world.

"Then let's get back home so you can finish all of your preparations," I said, moving toward the driver's seat of Masha's truck.

"I don't know what I would have done if you didn't come along." Totty waved her well-manicured fingers in the air. Shifting back and forth in her espadrille sandals, her bouncy bob shimmering in the truck's headlights, she looked eager to get off the highway and back to her family. "I'd probably be sitting in the cab of Moe's pickup with all that fabric until tomorrow morning."

I blinked. Something about her words didn't make sense.

"I thought you were picking up flowers," I said, letting my hand drop from the door handle.

I hadn't noticed it earlier, because I was too focused on rescuing her from the side of the road and getting back to Flat Falls so I could talk to Hollis. But Totty wasn't supposed to be getting the flowers for the ceremony. Ruby had been very specific about the design for the eucalyptus and succulent boutonnieres the gentlemen would wear during the ceremony. Nothing too flashy, she had insisted. And something that wouldn't wilt in the sun.

I interviewed five local florists before finding one creative enough to carry out her vision. Just that morning, I called him to confirm the delivery details.

"You must have misunderstood," she replied, a crease trying to form across a forehead that had seen far too many visits to the Botox clinic. "I'm just picking up a few bolts of fabric from the store so I can surprise the newlyweds with new curtains for their living room while they're on their honeymoon."

Even though I might have breathed in too much smoke or smacked my head too hard on the metal door of the food truck when it hit a speed bump, there was no way I'd misheard her.

Totty was lying.

My mind flashed to the pictures of the bonfire. My parents were holding hands, flanked on either side by their friends.

Rocky, Burton, and Wayne Daly on one side.

Moe and Beverlee on the other.

And in the middle, standing in the shadows next to Virginia Levi?

Totty Fowler.

Suddenly, the pieces started coming together.

She had always been there. Always in the background. Always inconspicuous. Even more invisible than Virginia.

And always wearing the same silver necklace.

I lifted the locket and held it to the light. "It's amazing how much history a piece of jewelry can hold. I still have my class ring. It's safe and sound in a velvet pouch in my nightstand. And every time I look at it, I can almost smell the sweat in the high school gymnasium."

"I wouldn't know," she responded, nervously winding her fingers through a piece of marsh grass she had plucked from the ground near Big Bacon's front tire. "I lost mine years ago."

"It's a shame to lose precious jewelry, isn't it? I know my mom would have been heartbroken to lose this one. All this time, I assumed it was at the bottom of the water. It's such a relief to know it was tucked away in Dad's pocket this whole time and that she didn't lose it during the accident."

"That locket meant the world to her. I remember when your mother bought it. It was a fundraiser they did for all the kindergarten parents—they made a killing playing on our emotions as we sent our babies off to school for the first time."

"That's right," I acknowledged, pushing aside the longing that tugged at my memory. I stepped around the front of the truck. "And didn't you have one just like it? With a picture of Ruby?"

"I can hardly remember what I had for breakfast this morning, Glory," she scoffed, her Southern drawl stretching the words out. "How do you expect me to remember what necklaces I wore nearly three decades ago?"

That was a fair point. I had never pictured Totty Fowler as a woman with a steel-trap mind. Instead, she was usually the one who'd have to leave the carpool line for a quick run to the Food Barn for the cupcakes she'd forgotten to buy for a class party.

"Why are you so worried about a silly piece of jewelry that probably went to the dump twenty years ago?" she asked, tapping her watch. "You know I'm in a bit of a rush. Can we reminisce about our old accessories later?"

I ignored her request and leaned my hand on the driver's side door, the locket clenched in my fist. "Hollis told me they found my mother's locket with Rocky's body, which made no sense. My mother adored my father, and there's no imaginable explanation for why that necklace was there."

"Glory, I don't know what you're—"

"But it wasn't her locket, was it?" The words spilled out before I could censor them, and even as the horror flashed in Totty's eyes, I couldn't stop myself. "So I guess the question is: why did Rocky Boyd have your locket when he died?"

"He... what?" The soft Southern lilt had disappeared from her tone, and her breaths came out in frenzied pants while her gaze darted around the area. "What would make you say such a thing? That's ridiculous."

All along, I had believed Rocky's killer was somebody obvious, somebody like Burton, who had a legendary temper and reason to suspect his best friend of making a move on his wife.

But that didn't explain who had been in that mobile kitchen and offed the chef in the middle of Ruby's wedding luncheon.

In my mind, the only person who connected the dots was Virginia. From the photos, it looked like she had been in love with Rocky, but if he had threatened to expose her to her husband, it could have easily tipped her over the edge.

I thought Virginia, with her folded hands and quiet platitudes, might have finally had enough of her culinary blowhard of a husband. Nobody would have blamed her, really. He kind of deserved it.

But it wasn't Virginia. At least not by herself.

"It was you," I murmured as all the details from the past week swirled together in my head. "Hollis said Rocky was having an affair, and because of the necklace, he assumed it was with my mom. But it wasn't. It was you. And I could see how people might get confused by the picture in the locket. Ruby and I both had brown hair and freckles."

"I don't know what you're talking about."

"Did you love him?" I knew how far a woman would go for the man she loved. Murder wouldn't have been on my list, but I could almost picture the desperation that could waltz a woman right off the deep end.

For a moment, her features hardened. Her hands blanched as she pressed them together. "I wish you hadn't done this, Glory," Totty said. "You've put me in quite a pickle."

She spun around, and I thought she would make a run

for it, but she just paced back and forth in front of the truck, the headlights illuminating her steps. She mumbled to herself as she moved, her arms frantically gesticulating as she gave herself a talking-to. Or a pep talk. I couldn't tell.

When she finally stopped marching, she turned back to me with a grimace. "I'm so sorry, honey. I didn't mean for any of this to happen."

With a sinking stomach, I realized that I hadn't given enough thought to the fact that if Totty had killed before, she wouldn't be afraid to do it again. When the small piece of metal in her grasp caught the reflection of the headlights, it was already too late.

A gun. Totty Fowler, the woman who stood next to the punch bowl for high-fives at every awkward school dance and the one who used cookie cutters on her sandwiches because she said ham and cheese tasted better if it was shaped like a dinosaur, was standing in the middle of the highway aiming a gun at my face.

"What are you doing?" My brain frantically searched for a way to rewind time. If only I hadn't stopped to help her, I would already be in Flat Falls, confessing to Hollis and well on my way to burying my anxiety in a fresh funnel cake.

I held out my hand, palm-first. I needed to calm her down, but first, I wanted answers. "Wait. Were you working with Virginia?"

I pictured some sort of bizarre, decades-long love triangle where Totty and Virginia were teaming up to bring down the men who had done them wrong. It was a made-for-TV movie just waiting to happen.

The gun wavered as confusion crossed her face. "Virginia? What does she have to do with this?"

"Uh… the library?" I answered, worried that I had to be the one to fill in the blanks for her. If she was going to be in cahoots with someone, the least she could do was keep up with the details.

"Oh, the fire," she said with a frenetic wave in front of her face like it was too difficult to remember all the intricacies of her double life as the PTA president and an arsonist. "That wasn't Virginia."

My fingernails scraped across the hood of the truck as impatience and fear battled inside me. "Then who was it?"

Totty stared out over the inky black water, her hand scrubbing at the back of her neck. "I never did like libraries. They smell like dust and disappointment."

"But I was in there!" Terror darted up my spine.

She took a quick step backward and whipped around to face me. "No, you weren't. There wasn't anybody there. I even made sure that assistant with the terrible perm had gone before I—"

"Before you what?" I shrieked, failing to keep my keep-the-woman-with-the-gun-calm voice under control. "Before you tried to kill me?"

"You've got it all wrong. You weren't supposed to be there. If you were back in Flat Falls doing your job, none of this would have happened."

"What could have been so bad that you needed to burn down a library?" I asked, hoping she couldn't hear the quivering in my voice.

"It's not..." Her words came tumbling out in a chaotic frenzy as her eyes frantically searched my face. "Virginia had something in there that I needed to dispose of."

"So you *set the building on fire?*"

She tugged at her shirt collar. "I'm so sorry, honey. I didn't mean to scare you. But those buildings are basically just tinder. You don't even have to go inside to light them up—just hide behind those big bushes along the front and bring along a little gasoline. So simple."

I'd keep that in mind for the next time I wanted to set a government building ablaze.

"Totty, put the gun down," I said, searching the area for something I could use to defend myself. "You don't want to do this."

I took a deep breath to steady myself, then stepped toward her, trying to figure out how to calm her down. Lying was my safest bet. "I'm sure the police will take that into consideration, Totty. They'll know this was all a big misunderstanding once we explain it to them."

"No, no, no. No police. The last thing Moe needs during an election year is a scandal."

Actually, the last thing Moe needed during an election year was a wife who took a swan dive off the deep end and tried to take out a city block with a pack of matches. "Of course," I replied, trying to keep my voice steady. "But I'm sure they'll sympathize, anyway. Things get stressful leading up to a wedding. Emotions run high. It's completely normal for the pressure to be too much. Everyone will understand—"

Totty clucked her tongue the same way she used to when I didn't finish my green beans when she had lunch duty in the elementary school cafeteria. "Oh, sweetie," she said, the lilt returning to her voice as she gathered her composure. "You don't need to be so dramatic. I really didn't know you were in the building, but now you've left me no choice but to handle it."

"Handle it?" My voice squeaked and I focused my gaze once again on the gun in her hand.

She motioned for me to move toward the bed of the pickup truck. "Moe keeps some rope back there. Won't you be a dear and grab it for me?"

I was going to say no, but then she waved the gun in the air like she was brandishing a trophy for lunatic of the year.

The tailgate dropped with a loud creak, and I tugged the coil of rope past the gas can, a stack of concrete blocks, and a weed trimmer. "Does your husband have anything to do with this?"

Totty snorted. "Moe? Heavens, no. He's probably back in his office practicing his father-daughter dance with our kitchen broom just to make sure he has the moves right for tomorrow. This wedding means the world to him."

"And what about you?" I tossed the rope at her feet. "You tried to kill me, Totty. Is that more important than Ruby's wedding?"

"I did no such thing. It was your fault you were in the library after hours." She shook her head as if rebutting my excuse for being late to ballet class. "And of course her wedding is the most important thing. She's my daughter."

"But she's Moe's daughter, too. Why would you risk…" I threw up my hands, wondering why Totty would do this. It made no sense. Unless…

"Moe isn't her father," I said softly.

Totty lurched forward, the gun inches from my face. "Bite your tongue. That man has been there for her since her very first breath. He's more of a father to her than Rocky Boyd ever could have been."

When she realized what she had said, she clapped one hand against her cheek, then used the gun in her other hand to point at the rope. "Oh, no. Look what you've done now. I'm so sorry, Glory, but I need you to pick it up."

Totty had always been one of those women who apologized for apologizing, but I had a hard time reconciling the sweet lady who had brought me homemade soup when I missed the fourth-grade zoo trip because of strep throat with the deranged woman teetering on wedge sandals on the sandy shoulder. I kicked at the rope with my toes. "What are you going to do, Totty? Tie me up and leave me on the side of the road? That's not like you at all."

"Of course not," she scoffed. "I'm not leaving you anywhere."

I swallowed against the lump of fear that had settled in the back of my throat. Totty wasn't pretending.

She was a killer.

Time ticked by for what seemed like hours when impatience made Totty smack the gun on the hood of Moe's truck, the metallic clang echoing off the water. "Pick up the rope. Now."

This time, her words weren't laced with Southern comfort.

I retrieved the rope and pressed the damp coil to my chest. "Now what?" I asked. Taunting the woman with the gun probably wasn't my smartest move, but if time had taught me anything, it was that you didn't get extra words on your tombstone for being nice. Nobody said, "Here lies Jane Doe. She always used her manners," so I'd be darned if I was going to sit by and let my classmate's mother murder me. She was a mom, not an assassin. In my mind, those two things were mutually exclusive.

If I was going to be judged for the rest of my life by what went down today, they were going to say, "That's Glory Wells for you. She went down fighting."

I took the rope and tossed it at Totty, hoping to knock her off balance, but she batted it away with the side of her forearm before lurching toward me. I spun around and tried to run, but the smoke and fear had dulled my reflexes. She lifted the gun and with a quick apology, smashed it against my head.

And the last thought I had before the blackness engulfed me, aside from the searing pain, was that I had underestimated Totty Fowler.

Everybody knew mothers were the strongest people around.

~

THE FIRST THING I noticed when I woke up was the smell of maple syrup. That was immediately followed by the realization that my behind was vibrating.

I pressed my fingers to my sticky forehead, the metallic scent of blood mixing with the sweetness to make my vision swirl. I felt unsteady, like I was floating.

I tried to lift my feet, but they wouldn't budge. And I wished somebody would turn off the music. The electric guitar riffs made my skull feel like it was going to break apart.

It took a moment of me glancing around to realize I was in the driver's seat of Masha's food truck, and the vibration was the revving of the truck's engine. But the front windshield was dark. There were no headlights, no street signs, no flashing emergency beacons.

The music sloshed in my head, an unrelenting chorus of oinks and electric guitar. I shook my head to clear my thoughts, but every movement made my body scream in agony.

I tried to remember what had happened, but I could only catch fragments of memory. Wisps of smoke. Flashes of terror. Water slapping my face with a force harder than concrete.

Water.

Icy panic shot through my chest, but I couldn't scream.

Everything stopped moving. Time. Space. Me.

When I finally had the sense to breathe, the music stopped screaming, and the engine stuttered to a halt.

My grip on the leather seat slipped.

So much blood.

Or maple syrup.

I couldn't tell.

But everything was wet. Salty and sticky, and when I went to wipe my hands off on the pants leg, I was met with a splash.

I shook my head. Blood didn't splash. Neither did maple syrup, except on those reality shows that included a kiddie pool and a bouncy model in a string bikini.

A wave smashed into my face, and the tang of salt hit my tongue. I instantly recognized the familiar taste of good, old-fashioned seawater. And from the looks of marsh grass that floated by my abdomen, it was seeping quickly into the truck.

I released my seatbelt, pain surging through my chest. But as I tried to push away from the seat, I couldn't. My feet were bound to the floor.

My chin dipped under the water, and I fumbled to grasp the rope that lashed my ankles to a heavy concrete block resting on the truck's long metal gas pedal.

Suddenly, the memories crashed down on me along with a torrent of seawater.

Totty Fowler tried to kill me.

More than once, if the thick knots around my ankles were any indication.

I jerked and heaved, but I couldn't loosen the binds.

Bone-chilling water undulated around my chest, rising higher with each passing breath.

I filled my lungs with two big gulps of air, then plunged my face into the water, my fingertips frantically working at the knots. I had never been good at tying knots, but I had spent more than my fair share of time flirting with a Boy Scout during freshman year. He would practice everything from bow lines to quarter hitches with me, and then he'd inevitably get called home for dinner, leaving me to extricate myself from yards of paracord while he ate his mama's Salisbury steak.

After sucking in half a bucket's worth of seawater, including what felt like a small fish, I freed myself from the ropes. But when I turned the door handle, the pressure from the water outside was too high, and I couldn't make it budge.

I kicked at the window and didn't have the strength to even crack it.

I watched as the flow of water moved through the truck, carried along by the rising water. When I let go of the seat, my body followed.

The current pulled me through a sea of pots and pans, finally propelling me toward a sliver of light that peeked through the open back door. I sent a silent prayer of thanks to Masha for never having that broken lock fixed.

Summoning my remaining strength, I kicked through the door, expecting to fight my way to the surface from the depths of the sea. I was surprised, though, when I ended up face-down in a boggy patch of marsh grass. I heaved myself up toward the bank, the Big River bridge illuminated above me by the night sky.

"Now why did you have to do that?" a high-pitched voice called out from the bridge. "If that stupid hunk of metal hadn't gotten stuck in the mud on its way down, you would be gone."

Thank goodness for trucks that didn't follow instructions.

"Totty, what did you do?" I belly-crawled through seaweed and dirt until I finally made it to solid ground. The truck had left a trail in the grass on its way down the hill from the road, and I used the reeds as leverage to hoist myself to the top of the embankment.

I glanced back over my shoulder at the truck, watching it sink lower in the mud and water with every passing second.

My body was dirty and soaked with seawater, and I smelled like three-day-old flounder topped with waffles. I swung a leg over the guardrail to face Totty, who was silhouetted against the headlights from Moe's truck.

"Why are you still here?" I asked, distressed that I had to face her again and wondering why she hadn't made a run for it while I was sinking to my doom.

She wrung her hands together as she stared down the highway, a puff of smoke from beneath Moe's hood reiterated that we were both stuck. "I'm waiting for someone to drive by and rescue me."

"Didn't think that through so well, did you?" One long shiver rolled through my body as the cold and adrenaline took over.

I didn't see that she still held the gun until she leveled it at my chest.

"You're not going to shoot me, Totty," I said, bravado fighting common sense inside my brain. "Why don't you give me the gun, so we can figure this out?"

Zing.

My mouth dropped as a single shot hit the concrete bridge barrier two feet to my left. "Totty!" I screamed. "What is wrong with you?"

Another shot bounced off the bridge. And this time, it felt even closer.

"You're not going to make this easy, are you?" She stepped toward me, gesturing with the gun as if it were an extension of her hand. "You're just like your mother, you know. Always so helpful. Right up until I had to jump out of the way of that truck, she was trying to figure out a solution to my problem."

"You… you were here?" I stuttered, losing my footing as surely as if she had shoved me. "When my parents died?"

She lifted a shoulder and motioned toward the edge of the bridge. "Your father's car was over there. We had a bit of a misunderstanding at Rocky's apartment, and I didn't want your parents going back to Flat Falls upset, so I followed them. It took me a while, but Daniel finally saw me flashing my lights and pulled over."

"What kind of misunderstanding?" I asked. "What did you want from him?"

Her patient smile sharply contrasted with the weapon she gripped. "You had a husband, Glory. You know how they are."

"What does this have to do with—?"

"Marriage is hard," she admitted. "And Moe and I haven't always had the best relationship."

Obviously, since she had just confirmed their daughter was fathered by another man.

"When we were first married, he spent a lot of time at the office, and I was… lonely."

I could sympathize. When Cobb and I were first married, I felt like I saw the pizza delivery person more often than I saw him. But that didn't mean I rushed out to entertain myself with another man.

"It was one night during a particularly busy campaign."

"And?" I prompted. "What does that have to do with my parents?"

"Your uncle was there for me when Cobb was too busy trying to get elected. Rocky paid attention to me, and… I let him."

I tried to contain an eye roll. "What was the problem, then? You wouldn't be the only woman to leave her husband for another man."

She whipped her head toward me. You would have

thought I'd accused her of wearing white after Labor Day. "You think I would leave my husband? For Rocky Boyd?"

"Then why were you chasing my parents? Why did you want to stop my dad that night?"

"He was going to tell Moe," she responded in a whiny whisper. "He was on his way back to Flat Falls to tell Moe that Ruby isn't his daughter."

"So you killed him?"

"No, of course not," she answered with a flippant wave. Her face displayed the level of remorse a normal person would show if they had dropped a piece of litter on the sidewalk. "Don't make it sound so theatrical. It was an accident. I just wanted to talk to him. I couldn't let him go back to town to tell Moe, not until I had figured out what I was going to do to keep Rocky from ruining everything. That truck came out of nowhere—it wasn't my fault."

"If it wasn't your fault, then why didn't you stay? You should have explained it to the police."

"What happened to your mom and dad was really sad, Glory. But it was that truck driver that hit them, not me. And I didn't stick around because I wanted to get back home to my family. Surely you understand that."

I felt like I was going to throw up. Bud never had a chance against this madwoman.

"What about Rocky, then? Did you 'not kill' him, too?"

"I didn't expect him to care so much, honestly. It was just one night. But after he found out that Ruby was his, he demanded to be a part of her life. Can you imagine?" She chuckled as if she was reliving a funny memory.

I wanted to pound some sense into her, to make her stop waving that gun around like she was the fairy godmother of Crazytown. But I kept my tone even, hoping to lull her into complacency so I could grab it away from her.

Plus, I was hungry. The only way I was getting back to Flat Falls to get a candied apple was if I knocked her to the ground and put an end to her deranged rant.

"How did he find out about Ruby?"

She cocked her head to the side. "Well, I told him, of course."

"What?" My own voice sent a knife through my skull.

She gave a noncommittal shrug. "When Ruby was about five, Moe and I hit another rough patch, and I wanted to see if Rocky had anything better to offer me."

Totty acted as if being married was like picking the best piece of pork at the meat counter. If she didn't like the one she had, she'd just select a better package, although I couldn't imagine any world where Rocky Boyd was the choice cut.

"I was in a bad place," she continued. "I thought he might want to run away with me."

"And did he?"

"No. And when he approached me the same night as your parents' accident, he said Daniel had convinced him that fatherhood was this wonderful adventure, and he owed it to Ruby to show up for her."

That, I could believe. There was nothing on Earth my father loved more than being a dad. Except for my mom.

"You can imagine my surprise when he showed up in downtown Flat Falls, threatening to tell Moe. He said he wanted to fight for his daughter—I just needed him to calm down long enough for me to talk some sense into him."

"And you calmed him down with—"

"My bumper," she responded matter-of-factly.

"Another accident?"

"Oh, no. I hit him like I meant it. I couldn't have him running off to tell Moe and ruining everything. Poor man dropped like he was made of hot pepper jelly, right there in the parking lot next to the new statue."

"And you decided to hide his body in there because they'd be filling it with cement the following day?" I guessed.

"Moe had been talking about the engineering of that statue for weeks," she admitted. "I knew there was a giant hole in the base just waiting for Big River Earl to be installed, which was a good thing, because I had no idea how heavy an adult man could be. If I had to drag that man any farther, it would have gotten ugly."

Uglier than murder?

"But I saw Rocky's postcard. He was at the beach."

Totty laughed. "Dragging a grown man across concrete in the dark is hard, Glory. Handwriting isn't hard."

Totty had been heralding the importance of penmanship and proper thank-you notes since I was in elementary school. And she had addressed hundreds of Ruby's wedding invitations with perfect calligraphy, so I wasn't surprised that she could fake a postcard from a degenerate.

Suddenly, headlights cut through the darkness. They were bearing down on us quickly, and I dove out of the way.

Totty didn't notice them until it was too late. She was standing on the bridge, right in the lane of traffic—just like she was on the night my parents were killed. Only this time, she couldn't jump out of the way.

The screech of tires and the scream of locking breaks blended with her hollow yowls as the large SUV careened into her.

∽

"DID YOU HIT HER?" A voice cut through the darkness. "I hope you hit her."

I would recognize that Southern drawl anywhere.

"Beverlee?" I yelled, crawling to my feet and lurching across the bridge.

Beverlee grabbed me in a tight hug. "Oh, baby, we were so worried. Are you hurt?"

I shrugged and motioned to the big SUV. "How did you find me?"

She yanked out her phone. "Bud heard something about a fire at the library, and we were worried you got caught up in the mess. So I used that tracking app I installed on your phone. Your dot was flashing in the municipal parking lot for half an hour, but when you disappeared, we decided that couldn't be a good sign."

My teenage self wouldn't have stood for such disrespect.

My adult self thought it was the nicest thing she had ever heard.

I pulled Beverlee in tighter, resting my head on her chest and not caring that I left a face-shaped mud print on her cream-colored blouse.

"It was Totty," I said, stepping back and motioning toward the woman who was sitting cross-legged at the side of the bridge while Scoots and Bud loomed over her. "She's the one who killed my uncle."

"We didn't know about Rocky," Beverlee responded. "But when Hollis came looking for her as a person of interest in Burton's death, we thought something strange was afoot."

"She killed Burton?"

Beverlee nodded. "Remember how terrible her black bean brownies were? She brought a batch to the luncheon and insisted she had made them just for Burton. And then she stood there and Southern-guilted him into eating one."

"She poisoned him?" I asked.

"They thought so at first, but it turns out she was just a

terrible cook. The brownies were so dry that he choked, and then when he was trying to get water, he slipped on the metal floor and conked his head on the corner of the prep counter. He tried to stand up, and she finished the job by clocking him on the head with a cast iron skillet. Then she just left him there, bleeding out with a batch of bad brownies stuck in his gullet."

"But why would she do that?"

"I don't know. Maybe Burton had something on her."

Realization hit me quickly. "Ruby."

"What about her?" Beverlee asked. "I don't think she had anything to do with this."

"Burton must have known the truth," I said with a resigned sigh. "Ruby isn't Moe's daughter. She's Rocky's."

"Why would it matter now, though? Rocky was long gone. What did Burton have to gain by pointing the finger at your father?"

I remembered the expression on Moe's face when he took the catering contract away from Ian. "Money. He must have blackmailed Totty into convincing Moe to give the town's contracts to Lavish. With the upcoming tourist season, that would be worth big money."

I let Scoots wrap me in a blanket from the back of Bud's SUV.

"So the rumors about Rocky having an affair with a married woman turned out to be true," I continued. "But it wasn't ever about my mother or Virginia. It was Totty all along."

Beverlee shot an approving glance at Totty just as sirens blasted from both directions. "Interesting. I didn't think she'd have it in her. But you know what that means, don't you?"

"That she's going to miss her daughter's wedding

because she's taking her Southern Crazy act straight to the state penitentiary?"

"Well, she is going to miss the wedding," Beverlee replied. "But it also means something else. You might not get that sister you've always wanted, but you did wind up with a brand-new cousin."

22

It came as no surprise the next morning that the Fowler family wasn't in the mood for a wedding. Finding out your mother is a murderer and your father isn't your father is a bridal buzzkill.

To top it all off, the groom didn't show up. Naturally.

According to Ruby's tracking app, he was somewhere in Mississippi with the brunette she saw on the sidewalk before helping me ram my car into the pig.

Although she was understandably upset, she finally admitted that it was for the best. Then she canceled his plane ticket to Saint Croix and upgraded her own to first class. "I need to get away from here," she said, "and there's no point in letting an exotic honeymoon go to waste." Since the resort still had Warren's credit card on file for incidentals, she also pre-paid for every spa treatment on the menu and ordered champagne and chocolate-covered strawberries to be waiting in the suite for her arrival.

On the morning of the planned ceremony, we gathered the bridal party, including Warren's mother, at Carolina Weddings. We surrounded ourselves with tiny shrimp quiches, mini cream puffs, and more than half a dozen full-sized cartons of Ben & Jerry's ice cream.

And since the town was counting on the publicity and revenue from the festivities, the tent had already been erected, and the coffers were stocked with fresh food from the Lavish kitchen, we had collectively come up with a solution.

"What time will the bride be here?" Virginia asked, popping a cheese cube into her mouth.

I glanced at my watch. "Beverlee was taking her to get cleaned up. They should be here any minute."

"It just might be the most romantic thing I've ever heard," Virginia said. "They'll get to live out their old age together, and it will bring our communities together."

"That feud has been going on for a hundred years," I admitted. "And despite all of our planning, I honestly don't think slapping up some tulle and offering free appetizers will be enough to stop all the fighting."

"Of course not," Virginia said, shaking her head. "But we're heading in the right direction. All we needed was a special bride."

"She's special, that's for sure." I swept my gaze around the room at Ruby's college roommates, who were touching up their lip gloss and taking photos wearing her veil. Since they didn't have anywhere else to go, Ruby had volunteered them to help with the festivities. "But she's going to need some bridesmaids. Are you guys up for it?"

A rousing chorus of agreement echoed through the room.

Just then, the bell above the door sounded, and Beverlee entered with a flourish. She placed Matilda's bedazzled cage on the floor, and more than one woman in the room let out a wistful sigh.

"Has anyone heard about the groom?" Virginia asked.

I checked my phone. "Bud and Scoots just got back from the formalwear store. They found a baby bow tie, and Phil Donahue is looking dapper and ready to see his bride."

Bud had finally gotten the nerve to ask Scoots out for a date, and although their first outing involved fishing the food truck out of the sound and enduring a police interrogation, it seemed to go well. He promised he'd take her to an actual restaurant the following weekend.

Scoots declined but suggested she might be up for some fried flounder takeout as long as she could wear her overalls.

I tried calling Ada to invite her to join us for the day, but she wouldn't answer my calls.

"You did rob her," Beverlee replied with a shrug. "Give it time."

I rested my hand on Virginia's arm. "How are you holding up? I know this is hard on you."

It turned out that Burton Levi had been buying restaurants all along the waterfront to help their struggling owners. As a child, he had watched his parents lose their restaurant, and he decided to buy the owners out before they had to watch their businesses fail.

He was going to turn one of the properties into a pay-what-you-can dining hall along the water. The other properties, he would sell and use the profits to help those local restaurants that could still be salvaged. Apparently, aside from blackmailing Totty for extra cash to put toward the cause once he figured out that she was the reason his best friend had spent the last twenty-five years stuck beneath a pig, he wasn't such a bad guy after all.

Totty had confessed to baking a batch of brownies to smooth things over with him but had spent the whole ride to the police station trying to convince Wayne Daly that the whole thing was an accident. Chief Daly happily handed her over to the Flat Falls deputy who showed up at the hospital because he said the women in our town were nothing but trouble.

Ian had finally gotten in touch with his friend Belinda, who confirmed that she sold The Crab Palace to Burton, not as a function of extortion, but to fund her move to Ohio so she could be near her grandkids.

Virginia admitted that although she would miss some things about her deceased husband, she was looking forward to discovering the world and running Burton's charity on her own. "You'll be happy to know that I've selected the first recipient of a gift from Burton's restaurant discovery fund. Masha will be getting a brand new food truck."

"She'll love that." I lowered my voice to a whisper. "But she wasn't his biggest fan. Are you sure that won't cause an issue?"

Virginia flitted her fingers in the air to dismiss the thought. "No, she was just mad because Burton never offered to buy her out. But he didn't need to—that breakfast truck pulls in five figures a month."

I let out a low whistle and wondered if it would be rude to leave the celebration to plan my next career as a mobile restauranteur. Since I knew how to drive the truck, I should be halfway to six figures already.

"We're also going to donate to the library to help with rebuilding after the fire," she said. "Although I can't believe you thought I had something to do with that. I'm a librarian, not a monster."

I returned her sheepish smile and said that Carolina Weddings would donate to the cause, too. It was the least I could do for throwing *War and Peace* against the wall.

"Dad also talked to the metalsmith who is making the new Big River Earl statue," Ruby added. "As a gesture of good faith and a measure of our commitment to goodwill with the people of Big River, he's going to commission two additional statues to sit next to the pig in the middle of the town square."

"Glory's mom and dad?" Beverlee clamped a hand to her chest, tears welling up in her eyes.

"That would have been nice, but no. Town center will now feature a statue of the newly married Matilda and Phil Donahue."

Ruby's eyes were puffy and rimmed with red, but she was determined to help with the days' events, despite her mother's face appearing all over the news. "It turns out that my parents haven't been happy together for years. Mom blamed him for being more focused on his political career than his family, and Dad said she gave up on him long before he became the mayor."

"But why now?" I asked, leaning against the front desk, munching on a broccoli and cheddar quiche. "What made Burton blackmail her all these years later?"

"When he discovered that Rocky hadn't skipped town after all, Burton started investigating on his own," Ruby answered. "Apparently he knew all along that she was unfaithful, but it wasn't until he listened to that answering machine tape again that he put the pieces together and confronted her about his death."

"And we know how that went," Beverlee supplied with a knowing nod. "That explains why Totty broke in and stole your box. I'll bet Burton mentioned the tape, and she thought it was here."

"I still can't believe my mother had so many secrets." Ruby sniffled, and at least three people offered her tissues before she brushed them away. "I know that I'll eventually have to deal with it, but I'm choosing to put it off until after my trip."

"Good plan," I replied. "And we'll be here to help you, because that's what families do."

After Totty was released from the hospital with minor scratches and taken into custody for Rocky's murder the night before, Moe and Ruby had spent the evening at Trolls nursing their broken hearts over baby pictures and two full pitchers of sangria. In the end, they both decided that no matter what the official paternity test said, he would always be her father.

Then he left town before the press could get wind of what had happened. But since his next campaign depended on the financial success of this wedding, before he hit the scandal-free highway, Moe begged Hollis to serve as his stand-in for the ceremony.

At first, Hollis declined the opportunity, but Beverlee cornered him with the promise of coffee and a handmade chocolate torte on her back patio. Then she reminded him that he falsely accused her only sister of infidelity when it was Totty and Rocky all along.

And whether it was from guilt or the promise of a semi-date with Beverlee, before he knew it, Hollis had become the official Justice of the Poultry.

A knock sounded at the door. We turned to see Hollis standing outside the glass, motioning to his watch.

He gave Beverlee a thumbs-up before turning back out to patrol the gathering crowd.

"That's our sign, ladies," I said.

We gathered Matilda in her tulle-wrapped cage and marched toward the wedding venue.

"Are you ready to get married?" I asked Matilda, sticking my pointer finger through her cage to pet her soft feathers as a show of sisterly support.

She promptly bit me.

I glanced over at Ruby, who was running her thumb

over a white satin sash from her bachelorette party. Thanks to a Sharpie that Beverlee had in her purse, it now read, *Not the Bride*.

"Ready, cousin?" I asked, giving my head a quick shake. Beverlee had been my only real family for so long that it was going to take some time to remember we were actually related.

Ruby gave me a hesitant smile and linked her arm through mine as we surveyed the crowd of about two dozen onlookers from both Flat Falls and Big River. They carried hand-painted signs showing their support for Matilda and Phil, and one bystander even suggested we add an anniversary parade to the Roadkill Jubilee every year.

After we re-named it, of course.

Beverlee tugged a tissue from her cleavage and dabbed her eyes. "Nothing brings people together faster than a wedding. But we're not changing the name of the festival. In fact, I'm going to make it a part of my campaign promises when I run for mayor in the fall."

She set Matilda's cage in the center of the stage next to Phil, who was dapper in his mini tuxedo. Then she scowled toward the crowd. "And if those folks from Big River don't like it, they can stick it where—"

I clamped my hand around her wrist. "Manners, remember?"

She simply smiled.

Because in the South, we're good at manners.

Most of the time.

∽

ACKNOWLEDGMENTS

The biggest gift an author can receive is the trust of her readers. When you curl up with one of my books, you're honoring me with your precious time, and I don't take that gift lightly. Thank you for allowing me to be a part of your lives.

I love being an author for so many reasons. One of the biggest is the team of experts who help me bring these stories to life. They're book people, too, and their dedication to excellence makes working with them a joy. Thank you to Mariah Sinclair, Virginia Carey, Stacy Juba, Kate Higginbotham, and Jana Hanson for being rock stars.

Writing a novel is sometimes a lonely endeavor, but I've been so fortunate to have the support and encouragement of some of the most talented and kind writers around, including Melissa Williams Pope, Gayle Trent, Liz Tully, Michelle Benningfield, and many others. Y'all are the best, and I love having you by my side for this writing journey.

A special thanks to my friends and family for believing in me and for the endless supply of socially distant high-fives. Mom and Dad, thank you for being my first readers and biggest fans. Thanks to Karen Brock for your friendship and for keeping me sane when the world went crazy. To Denny, Kathy, Diane, James, Kevin, and Jenn, Theresa, and Marcia, I couldn't ask for a better or more supportive pep squad. Thanks for making me laugh and for cheering me on.

Authors usually spend a lot of time alone, but I never thought I'd have to write a novel during a pandemic. For over a year, I wrote while surrounded by the kind of chaos only a big, rowdy family can provide. As a result, this book isn't just mine. It belongs to Sean, Miller, Gibson, and Serena, with my wholehearted thanks. You made lockdown fun and showed me we can do anything—as long as we're together. I adore you.

ABOUT THE AUTHOR

Erin Scoggins is a long-time Southerner with a fondness for offbeat humor and pickled okra. After fifteen years in marketing with a Fortune 500 company, she traded her MBA for fictional crime scenes and small-town scandals. She writes fun, flirty mysteries that are celebrations of food, family, and the killer South.

Craving something tasty? Nothing beats Beverlee's famous Bless Your Heart Cake.

Visit Erin at www.ErinScoggins.com/cookbook to get your free copy of *'Til Death Do Us Dine*, a collection of Southern snacks, sips, sweets, and stories to help you slay your next celebration.